A STAGE FULL
OF SHAKESPEARE
STORIES

WRITTEN BY ANGELA McALLISTER

ILLUSTRATED BY ALICE LINDSTROM

Lincoln
Children's Books

CONTENTS

Macbeth

Romeo and Juliet

Hamlet

A Midsummer Night's Dream

The Tempest

Twelfth Night

Othello

65

As You Like It

75

Julius Caesar

85

Much Ado About Nothing

95

King Lear

105

The Merchant of Venice

115

*"Double, double toil and trouble;
Fire burn, and cauldron bubble..."*

MACBETH

CAST OF CHARACTERS

Macbeth
A Scottish general and
Thane of Cawdor

Banquo
A Scottish general and
friend of Macbeth

King Duncan
King of Scotland

Lady Macbeth
Macbeth's wife

Macduff
A Scottish nobleman

MACBETH

One cold, wintry day, two figures riding across a wild Scottish moor. Macbeth and his friend Banquo were brave warriors returning from battle, weary after the fight that had won a great victory for their King.

As they made their way among the heather a grey mist swirled about them. Out of the gloom appeared three ragged figures, bent and gnarled as windswept trees.

"What are you, wild creatures?" asked Banquo warily.

"Speak if you can," demanded Macbeth.

Slowly, the figures let slip their black hoods, revealing the faces of three hideous witches. They raised their bony fingers and pointed at Macbeth.

"All hail to thee, Macbeth, Thane of Glamis!" they screeched. "Hail, Macbeth, Thane of Cawdor! All hail, Macbeth, who shall be King!"

Macbeth shuddered at the sight of the weird sisters. Their strange greeting disturbed him. How could they know his name and yet mistake him for the Thane of Cawdor? And what did they mean that he would be King?

"You seem to speak of the future," said Banquo. "What do you see there for me?"

The three hags turned to Banquo with crooked smiles. "You will be the father of Kings," they hissed, "but no King yourself!" Then before either man could speak another word, they snatched the mist about them and vanished.

"Don't trust what you saw," whispered Banquo as he and Macbeth continued on their way. "The strain of battle has weakened our minds. They said you would be Thane of Cawdor and wear the crown, yet both Cawdor and the King are alive and well."

At that moment a messenger came riding urgently across the heath.

"I bring thanks from King Duncan for your great victory," he told Macbeth. "You are to be rewarded with the title, Thane of Cawdor."

Macbeth listened in disbelief. "But the Thane of Cawdor is alive."

"That man is a traitor," explained the messenger. "He confessed to helping the rebels, so his land and title are given to you."

Macbeth drew Banquo close. "If one of the old hags' prophecies has come true," he murmured, "maybe the rest will follow!"

"Beware, my friend," said Banquo. "Dark powers often use tricks to lead men into wickedness."

Macbeth pulled his cloak across his chest and concealed the ambition the witches' words had sown in his heart. "Come," he said, "we must go to the King."

When Macbeth and Banquo arrived at King Duncan's palace they were greeted as heroes. Macbeth sent a letter to his wife telling her all that had happened.

Lady Macbeth read about the witches' prophecies with great interest. "Fate may need my help in this," she thought cunningly. "I know Macbeth longs for greatness, but he is an honest man. I must teach him to be ruthless and grasp the promised crown for himself."

Later that day, Macbeth returned home to his castle on Dunsinane hill. "King Duncan is to honour us with a visit tonight," he told his wife.

Lady Macbeth smiled. "This is your chance to fulfil the witches' prophecy, husband," she said. "You must kill the King while he sleeps. "

Macbeth was alarmed. "I cannot murder the King," he protested but even as he spoke his ambition grew.

"Where is your courage?" asked his wife. "Will you take the crown you long for, or live a coward for not daring to try?" Lady Macbeth used all her skills of persuasion, tempting and taunting her husband until, at last, Macbeth could no longer resist his hunger for power.

"I shall arrange everything," promised Lady Macbeth. "Just do as I say."

That night, Lady Macbeth gave King Duncan's guards a sleeping potion. When everyone in the castle was asleep, Macbeth slipped through the shadows to the King's chamber. At the door he saw the ghostly vision of a knife, floating before him. The sight of blood dripping from the blade filled Macbeth with fear. "Are you real or are you a dagger of the mind?" he whispered, but the only answer was the midnight bell. "Fate must have sent this vision to lead me," he told himself. So he entered the chamber, grabbed the knives from the sleeping guards and killed the King.

Next morning a cry of "Murder!" echoed through the castle. Lady Macbeth had smeared the guards with the King's blood to make it look as if they had killed him. Before anyone could question the guards, Macbeth, pretending to be shocked and angry, killed them both.

Everyone soon heard the tragic news. King Duncan's sons, Malcolm and Donalbain, were grief-stricken and afraid.

"We are not safe here," said Donalbain. "People may accuse us in this, for there are daggers in men's thoughts." So they left without delay. Malcolm hurried to England for the King's protection and Donalbain sailed to Ireland.

Many people soon believed that Malcolm and Donalbain had fled because they were guilty of the murder. With the heirs to the throne gone, Macbeth was crowned King, just as the witches had predicted.

However, one nobleman began to grow suspicious. Macduff, who had discovered the King's body, wondered why Macbeth had killed the guards without allowing them to be questioned and started to suspect that things were not as they appeared.

Banquo was also growing suspicious at how easily the witches' prophecies had come true for Macbeth. When Macbeth summoned all his nobles to a solemn feast to celebrate his coronation Macduff stayed away but Banquo could not refuse. Feeling uneasy, Banquo decided to take a ride with his son, Fleance, while the royal feast was being prepared.

Macbeth watched them ride away. Banquo knew what the witches had foretold. Would he

guess what Macbeth had done? And what did the witches mean when they told Banquo that he would be the father of kings? Macbeth's evil deed made him afraid and jealous of his friend. "My mind is full of scorpions," he cried. "I shall never be safe while Banquo lives." He ordered two men to follow Banquo and Fleance and kill them both.

Later that day, as the royal feast began, Macbeth heard the report that Banquo was dead but that his son Fleance had escaped and run away. Macbeth hid his displeasure with a smile as he greeted his guests.

However, when it was time to sit at the table, Macbeth was horrified to see Banquo's gruesome ghost, sitting in his place. Macbeth shrank away in terror. "You can't accuse me," he spluttered, pointing at the empty chair with a trembling hand. "Your blood is cold, your eyes have no sight. Be gone, horrible shadow!"

Everyone fell silent and stared at the King's strange behaviour.

"Don't be alarmed," said Lady Macbeth, "my husband often has visions like this." But the noblemen were disturbed by what they saw.

Now rumours and whispering began. People began to question King Duncan's death and Banquo's murder. Macbeth was haunted with such guilt and fear that he couldn't sleep. "I must find the weird sisters," he decided. "I have to know what my future holds."

The witches were waiting for Macbeth in a cave, lit only by the fire glowing beneath their bubbling cauldron. "By the pricking of my thumbs, something wicked this way comes," they chanted. Macbeth entered, eager to know his future.

From the cauldron's vapours the witches conjured up three visions. The first was the head of a soldier. "Beware of Macduff," it warned.

Then a child appeared, dripping with blood. "No man that is born of a woman shall harm you," it said.

Lastly, out of the gloom came a boy carrying a small tree. "You shall not be defeated until Birnam Wood comes to Dunisnane Hill," he promised.

Macbeth laughed with relief. "Every man is born of a woman," he said, "therefore I shan't be killed by any man. And a wood can never climb a hill, so it seems that I will die in my bed of old age!"

Macbeth returned to his castle, no longer afraid. A messenger was waiting with the news that Macduff had fled to England to join the old king's son, Malcolm. Macbeth was angry at this treachery. He ordered that Macduff's castle should be destroyed and all his family killed. "Let them plot," he jeered. "No man born of a woman can kill me!"

Macbeth's reign now became a time of terror as he wielded his power without fear. He trusted nobody and so everyone felt under suspicion. He took little care of his people, so poverty and hunger grew. Scotland longed for a just, wise ruler.

Several noblemen secretly promised their support to Malcolm. Swiftly he raised an army in England and began to march north with Macduff at his side. "We shall restore the crown to its rightful owner," Macduff promised, "and I will have revenge on Macbeth for the murder of my family."

Macbeth prepared his castle for a siege, still certain that no-one could threaten him. However, Lady Macbeth no longer had his strength of mind. Left alone in her chambers, she became tormented by memories of the dead King. She began walking in her sleep, trying to wash imaginary blood from her hands while muttering her guilty thoughts aloud.

Macbeth urged the doctor to cure her but there was nothing to be done. "Only your wife can rid herself of the troubles that cause this sickness of the mind," he said.

Although Macbeth's ambition had gained him the crown it had brought nothing else but

despair and death. As Malcom's army approached, he felt fate closing in on him, but he ordered his banners to be hung in defiance. Suddenly, a scream echoed through the castle. "The Queen is dead!" Her own dark deeds had overcome her.

Macbeth hung his head in sorrow but there was no time to weep. Strange news was sweeping through the castle. "Birnam Wood has come to Dunsinane!" voices cried.

"Liars!" shouted Macbeth, running to the window. But it was true, Malcolm's soldiers had disguised their number by covering themselves with branches from Birnam Wood and now they were moving up the hill.

"I've been tricked!" Macbeth called for his armour and led his men out from the castle to defend his crown.

Macbeth fought fearlessly, slaying everyone in his path. "Be afraid!" he cried as he wielded his weapon, "no man born of a woman can kill me!" Then above the sound of the battle he heard a familiar voice.

"Turn, hell-hound, turn!" It was Macduff. "Here is one who was not born, but taken from his mother's womb."

Macbeth was thunderstruck. He realised how the witches had deceived him. With a bitter laugh, he turned to face his fate. Macbeth threw his shield to the ground and raised his battle-axe. "Come then," he cried to Macduff. "Come, for I shall die like a warrior!"

"What's in a name? That which we call a rose
By any other name would smell as sweet."

ROMEO AND JULIET

CAST OF CHARACTERS

ROMEO
AND JULIET

Juliet
Daughter of Lord
Capulet

Romeo
Son of Lord
Montague

The Nurse
Nurse to Juliet

**Lord and Lady
Montague**
Parents to Romeo

**Lord and Lady
Capulet**
Parents to Juliet

Mercutio
Friend of Romeo

Tybalt
Lord Capulet's
nephew

Benvolio
Friend of Romeo

ROMEO AND JULIET

Long ago, in the Italian city of Verona, there lived two families who had been enemies for many years. The hatred between the Capulets and the Montagues was so strong that they often fought each other in the streets. One day, after a riotous brawl that upset the good people of the city, the Prince of Verona warned Lord Capulet and Lord Montague to control their families. The next person to disturb the peace, he told them, would be punished with death.

Not long after this, Lord Capulet arranged a masked ball and invited all the noble families of Verona. Lord Montague's son, Romeo, knew that his family wouldn't be welcome but his friend, Benvolio, had other ideas.

"I'm tired of seeing you mope around, sighing about your love for Rosaline," said Benvolio with a twinkle in his eye. "You know she doesn't care for you at all. Come to the Capulets' ball with Mercutio and me – when you compare Rosaline with the other beautiful girls you'll see she's really a crow among swans! You'll soon find somebody else to love."

Romeo couldn't resist. The Capulets' house was a dangerous place for a Montague but he longed to see Rosaline, no matter how little she cared for him.

On the night of the Capulets' ball, Romeo, Benvolio and Mercutio disguised themselves with masks. Romeo wandered among the guests, hoping for a glimpse of Rosaline but, unexpectedly, another girl caught his eye – a girl whose long, red hair gleamed in the torchlight. Romeo was mesmerised by her beauty. Gazing at her, he forgot all about Rosaline. He stepped nearer, his heart beating fast, willing her to notice him. When she did, she smiled shyly.

Romeo suddenly felt that nothing in the world mattered except the girl dancing gracefully before him. "I believe I never truly loved anyone until this moment!" he declared.

Unfortunately, Lord Capulet's nephew, Tybalt, was standing nearby and recognised Romeo's voice. "How dare a Montague enter this house!" he growled angrily. Tybalt pushed his way

ROMEO
AND JULIET

towards the door to fetch his sword but Lord Capulet stopped him and asked what was wrong.

"Our enemy Romeo is here," thundered Tybalt.

Lord Capulet remembered the Prince's warning. "Let him stay," he told Tybalt. "Romeo isn't causing any trouble. Although he's a Montague, people speak well of him."

"I won't watch that villain make a fool of us," Tybalt protested.

"If you won't obey me then it's you who must leave," replied Lord Capulet sternly. "I don't want a fight to ruin this evening."

Angry and frustrated, Tybalt left. "I'll not forget this, Romeo," he muttered under his breath.

Unaware of the trouble he'd caused, Romeo waited for an opportunity to speak to the girl with the long red hair. When the dance was over, he removed his mask and stepped close beside her. Gently he took her hand. The girl turned to him and blushed a little, her eyes wide with wonder. Romeo knew that she felt as he did, for she left her hand in his to tell him so.

"Does my hand offend you?" asked Romeo. "If so, my lips will kiss its rough touch away."

"Hands may touch to pray, as lips do," she replied.

"Then let our lips touch like our hands," said Romeo and he kissed her.

At that moment, an old woman interrupted them.

"Your mother wants to speak to you, Madam," she said. "You must go at once."

The girl let Romeo's hand fall. She gave him a radiant smile, then disappeared into the crowd.

"Who is she?" asked Romeo, watching after her in a happy daze.

"Surely you don't need to ask, Sir?" said the nurse with a frown. "That is Juliet, Lord Capulet's daughter!" And she hurried off after her.

"Juliet – a Capulet!" Romeo's heart sank. "She is my life, so my life belongs to my enemy!"

Suddenly, Romeo felt somebody tugging him by the arm. "Time to leave!" whispered Benvolio,

who had seen Romeo kiss Juliet. He led his love-struck friend away, hoping that nobody else had noticed.

On the way home from the ball, Romeo slipped away from Benvolio and Mercutio and turned back to the Capulets' house, where he climbed over the garden wall, into the moonlit orchard.

At that very moment, Juliet stepped out onto a balcony above. To her dismay, she'd just learned from her nurse that the handsome stranger at the ball was none other than Romeo, the son of her father's enemy.

"Oh Romeo, my love, why must you be a Montague?" she murmured, unaware that he was listening below.

Romeo stepped out from the shadows. "I'll give up that name if it's your enemy," he whispered.

Juliet was astonished and thrilled to hear Romeo's voice. She warned him of the danger he was in but Romeo wasn't afraid.

"I'd rather die now, at the hands of a Capulet, than live without your love," he told her. In hushed voices they spoke of their feelings for each other, talking happily until the first glow of dawn appeared.

Romeo didn't want the night to end. "I'm afraid to wake up and find that our love is just a dream," he told her.

"My love for you is real, Romeo," said Juliet. "If yours is too then let us be married, so we'll never have to part."

They agreed to marry quickly, in secret, so their families couldn't prevent the wedding. And so they parted, with the promise to meet at the chapel the following day.

Next morning, accompanied by her nurse, Juliet went to the chapel, where she and Romeo were married by Friar Lawrence. However, until the priest could find a way to tell their families, it was not safe for the young lovers to be together. The nurse promised to hide a ladder in the orchard so that Romeo could climb up to Juliet's balcony after dark.

Romeo was the happiest man in Verona that day as he went in search of his friends, Benvolio and Mercutio, to tell them his secret news. But as he greeted them in the square, Tybalt appeared.

"I've been looking for you, villain!" Tybalt shouted at Romeo. "How dare you enter the house of Capulet?"

"I'm no villain," replied Romeo breezily, "and I have every reason to love the name Capulet."

Tybalt drew his sword to fight.

"Let him be," cried Mercutio, "or I'll teach you a lesson."

But Tybalt was determined to punish the Montagues. He turned on Mercutio and the two began to fight.

ROMEO
AND JULIET

"Put your swords away, friends," insisted Romeo. "Remember the Prince has forbidden fighting in the street." Romeo grabbed Mercutio by the arms and held him back but, to his horror, Tybalt took the chance to thrust his sword into Mercutio's side.

"A plague on both your families," cried Mercutio, seeing blood pour from his wound. Benvolio took Mercutio in his arms, but there was nothing he could do to save him.

Romeo drew his sword. "One of us will die with him, Tybalt," he cried and he set upon Tybalt in a fury. With one fatal thrust, Tybalt was dead. Romeo dropped his sword and stared in shock at what he had done.

"Run, get away," urged Benvolio, "I'll explain everything." Romeo took one last look at his dying friend and fled, realising what a fool he had been.

A crowd quickly gathered and the Prince of Verona himself appeared. When he heard what had happened he was very angry. Benvolio assured him that Romeo had been trying to prevent a fight. "Then I shall spare Romeo's life," said the Prince. "However, he is banished from Verona for the life he took."

Meanwhile, Juliet waited with great excitement to see Romeo. She paced about her room impatiently, wishing the night would come. When the nurse arrived, Juliet begged her for news of him but the old woman's anguished face filled her with alarm.

"He's gone, Madam, gone!" the nurse cried. "Romeo killed your cousin Tybalt and now he's banished from Verona!"

Juliet was horrified. Was she wrong to have trusted a Montague after all? Knowing Tybalt's hot temper she guessed that he must have challenged Romeo. "I'm sure that if my cousin had not been murdered, my husband would be dead," she thought woefully. "I must see Romeo."

The nurse delivered a message to Romeo, who had taken refuge at the monastery with Friar

Lawrence. That night, as planned, Romeo came to Juliet's room, but instead of celebrating their marriage they comforted each other, knowing that he had to leave Verona forever. When the morning lark began to sing, Romeo promised Juliet that he'd soon find a way for them to be together. Then, with a heavy heart, he left her and set off for Mantua.

Later that morning, Juliet's mother came to her room and found her daughter in tears. "I bring good news," she said. "The noble Count Paris has long admired you, Juliet, so your father has given permission for you to be married."

Juliet stared at her mother in astonishment. "No, it can't be!" she gasped. "I won't marry Count Paris, a man I've never met." But she couldn't reveal the real reason why.

Lord Capulet was cross when he heard of his daughter's refusal. "You are lucky to be honoured by such a noble gentleman," he told her and insisted that the marriage took place that very week, before Paris changed his mind. In desperation, Juliet went to see Friar Lawrence, to ask for his help.

Friar Lawrence suggested a plan to reunite her with Romeo. It was daring and dangerous but Juliet was prepared to risk her life for her love.

Juliet returned home and told her father that she would marry Count Paris. Then, the night before the wedding, she drank a potion that the Friar had given her, which caused her to fall asleep so deeply that she appeared to be dead. When she couldn't be woken the next morning her family was distraught with grief. Juliet's wedding day became her funeral. With great sorrow, she was laid in the Capulet tomb.

Meanwhile, Friar Lawrence sent a messenger to tell Romeo that he should go to the tomb, for a day later, Juliet would revive and they could escape together. However, the friar's messenger visited a sick house on his way and found himself quarantined, unable to let anyone know that he'd been delayed.

Unaware of the plan, Romeo awoke late that morning with a smile. "I dreamt that Juliet found me dead, but her sweet kisses breathed life into me," he sighed happily.

Moments later, his servant, Balthasar, arrived from Verona, having ridden hard to bring the news of Juliet's death. Romeo listened in disbelief. Could it really be true? Balthasar nodded sadly. Heartbroken, Romeo shook his fist at the heavens. "Stars, I defy you!" he cried. "I won't accept this fate." He set off at once for Verona, stopping only to buy a bottle of poison to unite him with his love in death.

It was night by the time he came to the Capulet's tomb. With dread, Romeo stepped inside. Tears streamed down his face as he approached the coffin. When he saw Juliet's beautiful face so pale and lifeless his heart felt it would burst. "Forgive me, my love," he said softly. "I will never leave you again." Romeo pulled the poison from his pocket, drank it down and collapsed to the floor.

Moments later, Juliet stirred. Slowly, the colour returned to her cheeks and she sat up, drowsy from her long, deep sleep. As she blinked in the candlelight she saw Romeo's dead body on the stone floor, the poison bottle beside him. Juliet realised at once what had happened. She took Romeo in her arms and kissed his lips, desperately hoping to find some poison there for herself, but there was not a trace left. Then she saw Romeo's dagger at his side. Not wishing to live a moment more without him, she seized it. "Oh happy dagger!" she cried and she thrust the blade into her heart. Now at last, they would be together forever.

When the two lovers were found lying dead in each other's arms their families were filled with remorse. Joined in grief, the Capulets and the Montagues called an end to their fatal feud. The tragic love of Romeo and Juliet had brought peace to Verona at last.

ROMEO
AND JULIET

*"To be or not to be,
that is the question."*

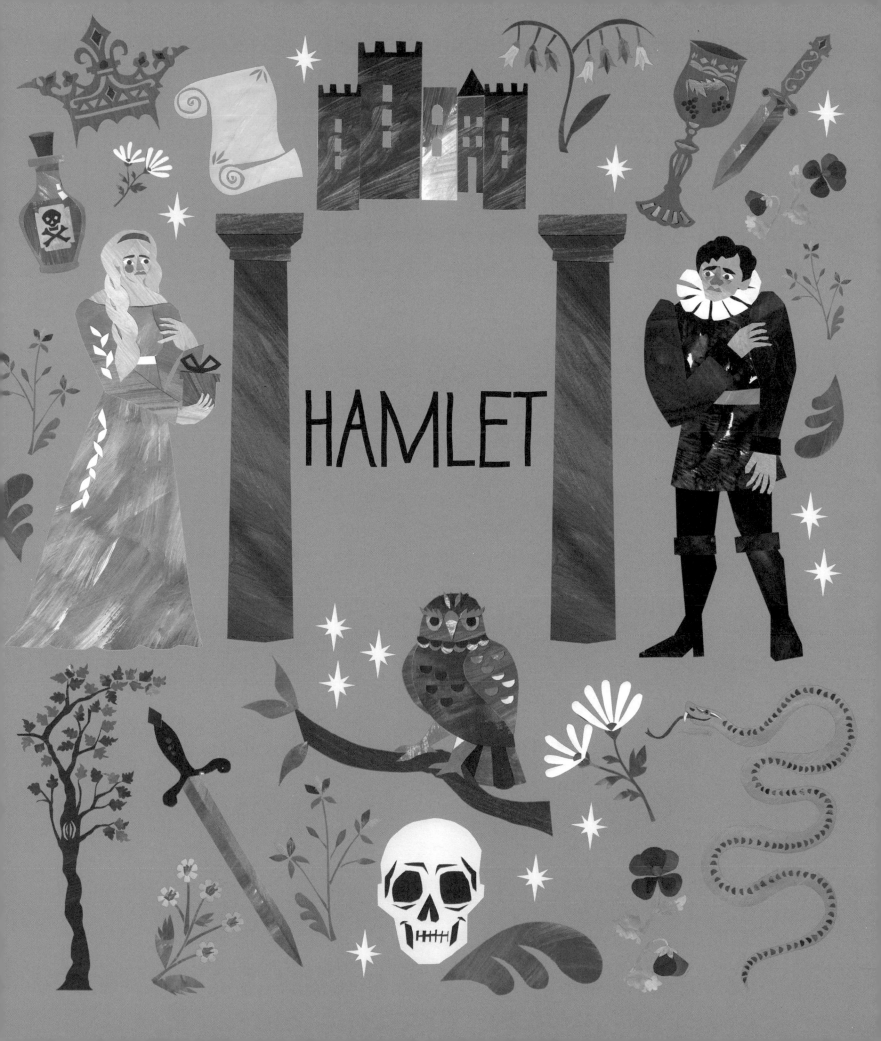

HAMLET

CAST OF CHARACTERS

HAMLET

Horatio
Hamlet's best friend

Hamlet
Prince of Denmark

Ophelia
Polonius's daughter

Gertrude
Queen of Denmark
Hamlet's mother

Ghost
Hamlet's father,
recently deceased

Laertes
Polonius' son
Ophelia's brother

Polonius
Chief counsellor
to Claudius

Claudius
King of Denmark,
Hamlet's uncle

26

HAMLET

HAMLET

It was a cold, starry night. High up among the rooftops of a castle in Denmark, Prince Hamlet and his friend, Horatio, waited for a ghost to appear…

For the last three nights, guards had seen a sad, eerie figure dressed in armour walk along the battlements. Now, Hamlet watched nervously to see whether the spectre was his dead father, the King.

As he shivered in the frosty air, Hamlet puzzled over the strange events of his father's recent death. He was still shocked that the King had died from a snake bite while sleeping in the garden. But it was even more disturbing that his mother, Queen Gertrude, had hardly waited a month before marrying again – to the King's own brother, Claudius. "Married before her tears were dry," thought Hamlet, hating his uncle for being so quick to wed her and claim the crown. Maybe tonight he would see his beloved father again…

Suddenly, the night air shimmered and a ghostly figure in silver armour appeared. It moved slowly, without a sound, and beckoned Hamlet close.

Hamlet's heart thudded in his chest. When the ghost raised its visor he saw his father's face, pale as moonlight and full of sorrow.

"Hamlet, my son," said the ghost gravely. "It was no snake that killed me. Your uncle Claudius poured poison into my ear. He murdered me without a chance to say my prayers, then he took my queen and my crown."

Hamlet was filled with anger. He'd been right to mistrust his treacherous uncle.

"If you love me, Hamlet, avenge my murder!" cried the ghost.

"I will, Father," promised Hamlet. "Claudius shall pay with his life for what he has done!"

"Then fare thee well, Hamlet," said the ghost. "But take care not to blame your mother. Let heaven be her judge." And with a deep sigh, he faded away like a breath in winter.

HAMLET

Hamlet and Horatio agreed not to tell anyone what they'd seen but Hamlet was haunted by his terrible secret. If only he could have turned to Ophelia, the gentle girl he'd grown to love before he went away to university. But since his return, Ophelia had refused to see him. Hamlet didn't know that she'd been forbidden to speak to him by her father, Polonius, who feared that a Prince could never truly love a girl who wasn't of the same noble birth. In Hamlet's eyes it seemed that Ophelia didn't love him anymore. Feeling betrayed by everyone around him, he now wondered who he could trust.

Day after day, Hamlet struggled to decide what to do. All he could think about was his promise to avenge the King's murder. Could he believe the ghostly apparition? Maybe it was an evil spirit wishing to tempt him? He had to be sure before he could act.

Hamlet's mind became so full of turmoil that he hardly ate or slept and the more exhausted he became, the more strangely he behaved. He brooded about, unshaven and dishevelled, talking out loud to himself. People whispered about him. "They think I've gone mad," Hamlet thought but this gave him an idea. "Let them believe it," he decided. "No one will suspect a mad man while I search for proof of the ghost's words – that Claudius killed the King!"

So Hamlet began acting the madman; one minute talking foolish nonsense, the next minute miserable with grief. But no matter where he lurked and listened, he couldn't find proof of his father's murder. "Do I have the courage to keep my promise to the ghost and kill my uncle," he thought, "or should I do nothing and live with that hateful traitor, Claudius, as my stepfather and King?"

His dilemma troubled him so deeply that Hamlet started to wonder if the only way to escape from his torment was to put an end to his own life. "To be or not to be?" he asked himself. What was the answer?

HAMLET

The King and Queen became worried about Hamlet's changing moods.

"I'm sure this madness is caused by the death of his father," said Gertrude but Polonius, who was the King's chamberlain, suggested another explanation.

"The Prince has been showing affection for my daughter, Ophelia," he told the King and Queen. "I advised her not to encourage him but I think it's her refusal that has driven him mad." Polonius offered to arrange a meeting between Ophelia and Hamlet so that the King could secretly observe their behaviour for himself.

The next afternoon, to Hamlet's surprise, he found Ophelia waiting for him. "I've come to return the gifts you gave me," she said sadly.

Hamlet gazed at her fair face but he no longer trusted her. "Ophelia's father is too close to my scheming uncle," he thought to himself so he pushed the gifts aside. "I once said that I loved you, but you should not have believed me," he told Ophelia. "I loved you not."

Broken-hearted and confused, Ophelia burst into tears. "Have no thought of marriage," Hamlet continued. "Of those that are married, all but one shall live!"

"Oh, I am the most miserable of women!" cried Ophelia and she ran from the room.

HAMLET

As planned, Claudius had been secretly listening nearby. Hamlet's words made him suspicious. Was his stepson really mad or had he guessed Claudius's secret? He decided to send Hamlet away. "A sea voyage to England should bring the Prince to his senses," he told Polonius.

"Ask the Queen to talk to Hamlet alone first," suggested Polonius. "Maybe he will open his heart to his mother. A play is arranged for your entertainment this evening. Afterwards, I will spy on their conversation and report it to you." Claudius agreed.

Later that day, as the travelling actors prepared for the play they were to perform, Hamlet went in search of Horatio. He urged his friend to attend the performance that night. "I've given the actors new lines that change the play so that now it will imitate my father's murder," Hamlet explained. "Watch Claudius closely as the play unfolds. We'll see if the ghost spoke the truth. The play's the thing to catch the conscience of the King!"

That evening, Claudius paid little attention as the performance began. But when the players acted out a murder, pouring poison into the ear of a sleeping King, Claudius leapt to his feet. "Enough! Get out!" he shouted angrily and he stormed out of the room. The whole court followed, mystified at the King's behaviour. Only Hamlet and Horatio remained.

"Did you see his guilty face?" asked Hamlet.

"There can be no doubt," Horatio agreed.

Shortly afterwards, Hamlet received a message from the Queen asking him to come to her room. On his way to the Queen's apartments Hamlet paused at his uncle's door. "I have the proof now," he thought. "Here is the perfect opportunity to avenge my father." But to Hamlet's

dismay, he found Claudius on his knees in prayer, shaken by what he had seen in the play. Hamlet held back. "If I kill Claudius now he will find forgiveness in heaven," he thought with exasperation. "I must wait for another chance to send him to the devil for his deeds."

Hamlet left silently and went on to the Queen's room. Although he'd promised the ghost that he wouldn't punish her, Hamlet was determined to confront his mother with the truth. "I will speak daggers to her," he told himself, "but I will use none."

Queen Gertrude was waiting in her chamber. "Hamlet, you have offended your uncle," she told him.

"Mother, you have betrayed my father!" he replied.

Gertrude was suddenly frightened by the look of madness in Hamlet's eyes. "I fear you have come to murder me," she cried. "Help! Guard!"

"Help! Guard!" echoed a voice from behind the curtain. Hamlet swung round, thinking that Claudius must have slipped into the room to eavesdrop on their conversation. "Now here's a chance to punish my father's murderer!" he thought to himself and he drew his sword and thrust it through the curtain. But to his horror, Polonius slumped to the floor at his feet, dead.

HAMLET

Polonius's death gave Claudius the perfect excuse to send Hamlet away from Denmark. "The Prince's madness is a threat to us all," he told Gertrude. "We must send him to England for our safety and his own." Claudius didn't tell the Queen that he would also send a letter, ordering that Hamlet be murdered when he arrived.

Hamlet had no choice but to obey the King. However, his ship was not destined to reach England. After only a few days at sea it was attacked by pirates. The Prince offered the pirates a reward to return him to shore, but there, he found himself far from home.

Hamlet made the long journey back to the castle. When he finally arrived, he saw Gertrude and Claudius leading a funeral procession into the graveyard. They had come to bury Ophelia, who'd been so distressed by Hamlet's rejection and her father's death, that she had drowned in a stream.

Beside the grave stood Ophelia's hot-headed brother Laertes, recently returned from his travels in France. Laertes had been told by the King that Hamlet was responsible for the deaths of his father and his sister, so when he saw Hamlet he lashed out at him angrily. "The devil take your soul, Prince!" he cried.

But Hamlet could only stare at the coffin strewn with flowers that lay before him. "I loved Ophelia," he said tearfully. "Forty thousand brothers could never match my love."

Claudius was alarmed by Hamlet's return. He set about devising a new plan with Laertes to get rid of him. The King arranged a fencing match between the two young men. No one else knew that he'd given Laertes a poisoned blade and prepared a glass of poisoned wine for Hamlet in case the blade should fail.

Everyone at court gathered to watch the fencing match. Horatio was worried for his friend but Hamlet was unafraid. "If I am to die today, Horatio, I am ready," he said.

The match began. Hamlet was the most skilful opponent and soon scored the first hit, prompting praise from the King, who offered him the poisoned wine as a toast. But Hamlet wasn't ready to drink. To the King's horror, Gertrude drank from the glass instead. Knowing nothing could save her, Claudius let the match continue. Hamlet was scratched by Laertes' rapier and then, in a scuffle, both weapons were dropped and switched hands. In an instant, Hamlet wounded Laertes with the poisoned blade.

At that moment the Queen was overcome. "The wine…" she gasped. "I've been poisoned!" And she fell dead to the floor.

Laertes hung his head. "That blade has poisoned us too, Hamlet," he confessed. "We have little time to live. The King's to blame!"

Everyone stared with shock at the King. "Treason!" they cried.

Claudius rushed for the door but Hamlet shouted for it to be locked so that he couldn't escape. Feeling his strength already ebbing away, Hamlet stabbed Claudius with the poisoned rapier, then he seized the glass of poisoned wine and forced his wicked uncle to drink. "Venom, do your work!" he cried.

The promise to his father's ghost fulfilled, Hamlet sank into Horatio's arms.

"Sleep well, sweet Prince," murmured Horatio.

"Remember to tell my story, loyal friend," whispered Hamlet. And, with that, the Prince of Denmark died.

"If we shadows have offended,
Think but this, and all is mended,
That you have but slumbered here
While these visions did appear…"

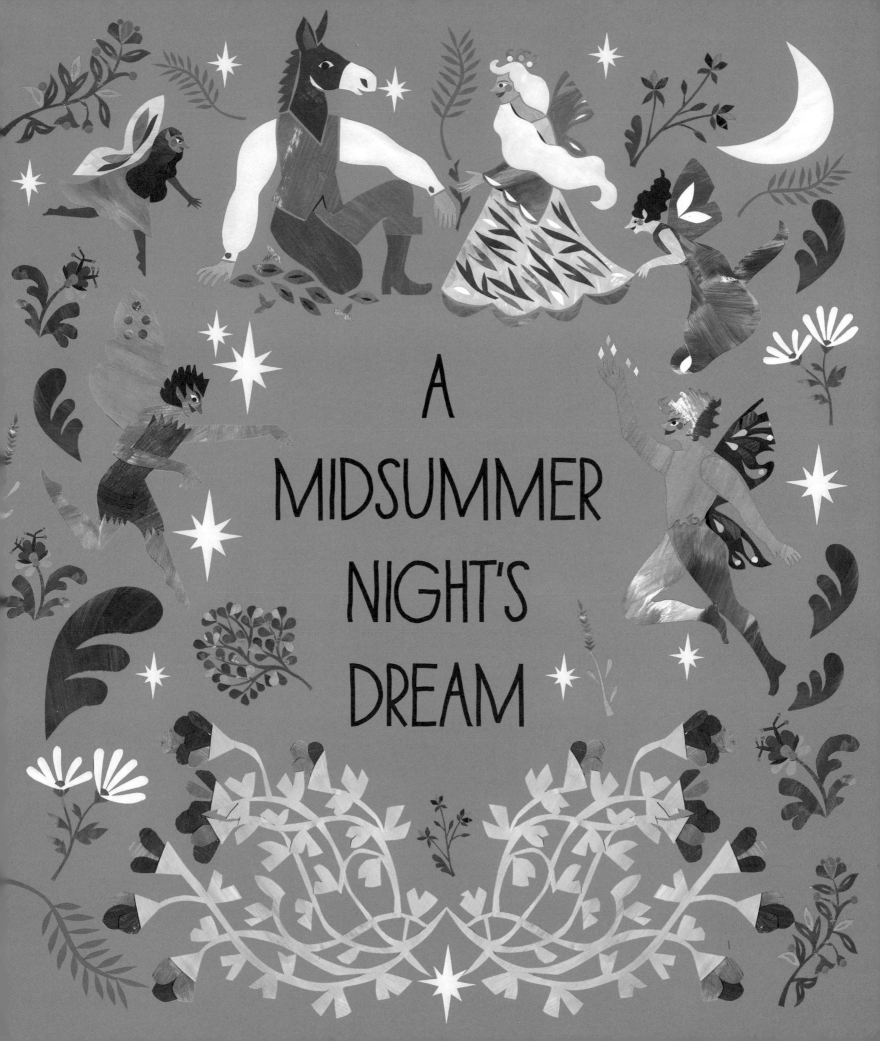

A
MIDSUMMER
NIGHT'S
DREAM

CAST OF CHARACTERS

A MIDSUMMER NIGHT'S DREAM

Hermia

Lysander

Puck
Fairy servant of
Oberon

Oberon and Titania
King and Queen
of the fairies

Bottom
A weaver

Theseus

Helena

Demetrius

A MIDSUMMER NIGHT'S DREAM

A MIDSUMMER NIGHT'S DREAM

In the beautiful Greek city of Athens, Duke Theseus was soon to be wed to the Amazon Queen, Hippolyta. The city bustled with wedding preparations but not everyone was happy. Pretty, blue-eyed Hermia was in love with a young man called Lysander but her father wouldn't allow them to marry. He insisted that another man, Demetrius, would be a better husband. No matter how much Hermia protested, her father refused to change his mind.

Raven-haired Helena was also sad. She'd been engaged to marry Demetrius herself before he met her friend Hermia and she'd never stopped loving him. However, she cheered up when she heard that Hermia had a plan.

"Tonight, Lysander and I are going to meet in the wood outside Athens and run away together," Hermia told her. "When we're gone, Demetrius will soon forget me and you can win him back for yourself."

The girls wished each other luck and said goodbye. Helena's heart beat fast. "If Demetrius hears about Hermia's plan from me first I'm sure he'll be grateful," she thought, so she decided to tell Demetrius straightaway and remind him of her own faithful love.

When evening came, Hermia and Lysander slipped away from the city. But they weren't the only ones in the moonlit wood that night. Fairies appeared among the silvery trees. Oberon, King of the fairies and his wife, Queen Titania, were quarrelling. Titania had adopted a young boy but the attention she gave him had made her husband jealous.

"Give the boy to me," demanded Oberon. "He can be my attendant."

Titania fluttered her shimmering wings. "No, Oberon," she answered. "I won't part with him, not for all your fairy kingdom!" The two argued until, at last, Titania refused to discuss the matter any further. She beckoned to her fairy maids and left to find a place to sleep.

Oberon was cross with his defiant wife. "Go your own way," he muttered, "but you won't leave this wood, my Queen, until I've taught you a lesson."

Oberon called for his lively sprite, Puck, who always delighted in making mischief. "Fetch me the magic flower they call Love-in-idleness," he asked. "A drop of its juice on the Queen's eyelids will make her love the first creature she sees when she awakes."

Puck grinned at the thought of some trouble-making. With a bow to the fairy King, he darted away on his quest.

While Oberon waited for Puck to return he amused himself by imagining what creature would capture Titania's heart when she awoke. "Will it be a lion, or a bear?" he wondered. "Whatever it is, I won't remove the charm until she loves me more than her precious boy."

Just then, Oberon heard voices nearby. He made himself invisible. Demetrius had come to the wood to search for Hermia. To his annoyance, Helena was running after him.

A MIDSUMMER NIGHT'S DREAM

"Go home, Helena," said Demetrius sharply as he pushed his way through the bushes. "Stop following me, I don't care about you any more." But Helena wouldn't leave.

"I still love you, however hard-hearted you are," she vowed as she scrambled along behind him.

The two hurried on down the path, unaware that the fairy King had heard every word.

Oberon felt sorry for Helena. When Puck returned, he told him about the young couple from Athens. "When they stop to rest, drop some flower juice onto the young man's eyes, so that he'll love the maiden when he wakes," said Oberon. Then he took some of the magical juice himself and flew to the glade of rambling roses where Titania was asleep.

Oberon gently squeezed the flower juice onto the Queen's eyelids and whispered:

"Whatever you see when you awake,

For your dearest love you'll take,

Be it lynx or cat or bear,

Leopard or boar with bristly hair!"

Then, smiling to himself, he slipped away.

Nearby, Hermia and Lysander had wandered for several hours together in the wood and were now lost.

"You're tired, my love," said Lysander. "Let's sleep here tonight. It will be easier to find our way out of the wood in the morning.

Hermia agreed. With a yawn, she laid down among the sweet-scented flowers. Lysander didn't want to leave her side, but as they weren't yet married, he found himself a mossy bed a little way off and they were both soon fast asleep.

Along came Puck. "This must be the young man from Athens that Oberon sent me to find," he thought. "And there's the pretty young maid he shall learn to love when he wakes." Quick as a hummingbird, Puck dripped the magic juice onto Lysander's eyelids and danced away.

Moments later Demetrius strode through the trees, still followed by Helena.

"Stop, Demetrius," she begged. "I'm exhausted!" But he ignored her and walked on.

"I give up," Helena sighed miserably, pulling the brambles from her dress. She watched

Demetrius disappear into the shadows. "Why should he look at me when he loves Hermia's pretty face? I'm as ugly as a bear."

Then, to her surprise, she noticed Lysander lying on the grass. "This is strange," she thought and she shook him gently to wake him.

Lysander opened his enchanted eyes. At once he fell deeply in love with Helena.

"Where is my rival Demetrius?" he asked. "I shall kill him with my sword!"

Helena was alarmed. "You don't need to fight Demetrius," she told him. "Hermia doesn't care about him, she loves you."

"Hermia?" Lysander frowned. "I regret the boring hours I spent with her. It's you that I love, Helena." He took her hand and kissed it tenderly. "Who wouldn't change a raven for a dove?" he sighed.

Helena thought he was making fun of her. "What have I done to deserve this mockery?" she cried. "It's bad enough that Demetrius hates me and now you tease me too!" Feeling wretched, she burst into tears and ran away with

Lysander hurrying after her.

Disturbed by the noise, Hermia awoke and called out for Lysander. But to her surprise, she found herself alone. "Why would he leave me?" she wondered. Without a clue as to where he'd gone, she set off in search of him.

While the four young people hunted for each other in the wood, a group of craftsmen met in a grassy clearing. They'd come to rehearse a play, which they hoped to perform at the Duke's wedding celebrations.

Bottom, the weaver, was full of his own importance and keen to play every part. But Quince the carpenter took charge. "Wait behind the blackberry bush, Bottom, until it's your turn to speak," he told him.

Puck heard their voices and crept close to see what was going on. Knowing that Titania was sleeping nearby, he saw a chance to have some fun.

Puck crept over to the blackberry bush and whispered a magic spell. When it was Bottom's turn to speak he stepped out, unaware that he now had the head of an ass. His friends stared in horror. "The wood is haunted!" they cried and they ran away in terror.

Bottom paced up and down, wrinkling his whiskery nose. "I see what they're doing," he told himself. "They're trying to frighten me, to make an ass of me. Well, I'll show them that I'm not afraid of being alone in a dark wood." And he began to sing.

A MIDSUMMER NIGHT'S DREAM

Bottom's song ended with a loud "hee-haw!" which woke up the fairy queen. Under the spell of the magic flower juice, she gazed at his hairy head and long, shaggy ears and fell deeply in love with him.

To Bottom's delight, beautiful Titania led him to her flowery bed. There, her fairies hung a garland of rosebuds around his neck and fed him fruit and honey, while Titania stroked his nose and whispered words of love in his ear. "At last, someone who appreciates me," sighed Bottom happily.

Puck hurried away to tell Oberon, who was delighted to hear how well his charm had worked. "And did you find the young man from Athens?" Oberon asked.

Puck nodded. "All is done," he said.

Suddenly, they heard rustling nearby. Demetrius and Hermia appeared.

"Watch now, here is the young man himself," whispered Oberon.

"But that's not the one whose eyes I

charmed," murmured Puck.

Hermia's eyes were red with tears. As she couldn't find Lysander she thought that Demetrius must have killed him in a fit of jealousy. "There can't be any other explanation," she said angrily. "You found him asleep and murdered him!"

"How can you be so cruel to me when I love you?" protested Demetrius. "I'm not a murderer. I'm sure Lysander is alive somewhere."

But Hermia was certain that Lysander would never have abandoned her. "I hate you, Demetrius!" she sobbed. "Whether Lysander is alive or dead, you'll never see me again," and she ran away into the trees.

Demetrius sat down, exhausted and fed up. "There's no point following Hermia while she's in such a fierce mood," he thought to himself, so he lay on the grass to sleep awhile.

"We must put this right," Oberon said to Puck. "Find Helena and bring her here, while I use the magic charm once more."

A MIDSUMMER NIGHT'S DREAM

Oberon squeezed a drop of flower juice onto Demetrius's eyes but before Puck had been gone a moment, Helena appeared, looking very upset, with Lysander at her heels.

Lysander was still trying to persuade Helena that he loved her. "Why do you think I'm teasing you?" he asked, gazing at her adoringly.

"Because you vowed to marry Hermia," snapped Helena in exasperation.

Their voices woke up Demetrius. To everyone's surprise he jumped to his feet and grasped Helena's hand. "Oh, perfect goddess, my love," he sighed. "Nothing can compare to your crystal eyes, your cherry lips and your skin as white as snow."

Poor Helena couldn't believe her ears! She tugged her hand away. "Don't be so mean, Demetrius," she said. "What have I done to make you both mock me like this?"

Lysander turned to Demetrius. "Everyone knows you love Hermia," he said. "Well, now she is free. I wish to devote my life to Helena."

"You can keep Hermia," replied Demetrius scornfully. "My heart was only a guest with her, now it has returned home to Helena forever."

When Hermia heard Lysander's voice she came running to find him. "Why did you leave me, my love?" she asked. "I was alone and afraid."

But Lysander didn't even look at her. "I follow Helena, who brightens the night more than all the stars," he replied.

Hermia stared at him in astonishment. "Surely you don't mean what you say?" she gasped.

Helena looked at her suspiciously. "Did you encourage Demetrius and Lysander to tease me?" she asked. "They'd both do anything to please you. I thought you were my friend."

Hermia shook her fists in frustration. "You are no friend of mine, Helena!" she cried. "You must have crept up in the night and stolen Lysander's heart!" She was so angry that Helena feared she would scratch out her eyes.

Insults and accusations flew back and forth until Demetrius and Lysander stormed off to find somewhere to fight and Helena, afraid to stay a moment longer with Hermia, fled away into the night.

Puck chuckled with glee. However, Oberon was not amused by all the uproar and unhappiness. "This is your fault," he told Puck sternly, "and you must put it right."

With a shrug, Puck agreed. He flew up into the sky and pulled a veil of dark clouds across the moon and stars. Then he led the four young people blindly through the wood until they

A MIDSUMMER NIGHT'S DREAM

were so tired that they fell asleep. With a magic herb he removed the charm from Lysander's eyes so that he would love Hermia once more when he awoke.

Later that morning, Duke Theseus and Hermia's father rode into the wood together. They were surprised to find Hermia and Helena sitting among the flowers with the two rivals, Lysander and Demetrius. All four were smiling happily, full of wonder at their curious dreams.

"By some strange power my feelings for Hermia have melted away," said Demetrius. "Let her marry Lysander, it is Helena that I love." Helena, who had forgotten all her doubts, flung her arms around him. Hermia's father, relieved to see harmony at last, heartily gave his consent and Duke Theseus congratulated them all.

"So, there shall be three weddings today in Athens," said the Duke. "I invite you all to share my celebrations."

A short while later, as the joyful couples returned to the city to make their preparations, Bottom woke up. "What an odd vision I had," he said, scratching his ear. "Well, I won't make an ass of myself by telling everyone about it." And, brushing the rose petals from his hair, he set off home.

Everyone in Athens was in a merry mood that midsummer wedding day and no one laughed louder than the Duke when Bottom and his friends performed their play.

Oberon had removed the charm from Titania's eyes and their quarrel was forgotten. Happily in love once more, the fairy king and queen cast a spell to bless the newlyweds, so that not even mischievous Puck could disturb them from living happily ever after.

"Be not afeard. The isle is full of noises,
Sounds, and sweet airs that give
delight and hurt not."

THE TEMPEST

CAST OF CHARACTERS

Alonso
King of Naples

THE TEMPEST

Miranda
Prospero's daughter

Prospero
Former Duke of Milan

Caliban
Prospero's servant

Ariel
Sprite on the island

Ferdinand
Alonso's son

A court jester

A drunken butler

46

THE TEMPEST

THE TEMPEST

Prospero the wizard stood among the sand dunes of a wild, windswept beach, watching a ship sail into view.

"At last, fate has brought me a chance to right the wrongful deeds of the past," he thought to himself. "My refuge on this island will soon be over." He stepped down to the water's edge, raised his magic staff and called up a storm. At his command, thunderclouds darkened the sky, lightning flashed and the sea erupted like a waking monster. Towering waves tossed the ship towards the rocky coast.

On board, King Alonso of Naples and his son, Ferdinand, were seized with terror. "What's happening?" they cried.

"If we stay here, we shall all be dashed to pieces," shouted their companion Antonio, the Duke of Milan. Fearing for their lives, the noblemen leapt into the churning sea.

Prospero's daughter, Miranda, came running to his side. "Father, don't use your magic this way," she pleaded. "A ship will be wrecked and lives will be lost."

Prospero lowered his staff. At once, the storm rolled away and the sea grew calm again but the ship was nowhere to be seen. "Have no fear," he told Miranda. "No-one has come to any harm. I have done this for you."

Miranda was puzzled by her father's words.

He took her hand. "There are things I must explain," he said gently. "It is time to tell you who we are and how we came to this island." Miranda sat with him on the sand, eager to know more.

Prospero told his daughter that he was once the Duke of Milan. "Long ago, we lived in a beautiful palace with a great library, where I loved to spend time with my books of ancient magic," he said. "As I was devoted to my studies I trusted my brother, Antonio, to run the

affairs of state. However, Antonio enjoyed his power too much and grew ambitious. When you were only three years old, he made a secret deal with my enemy, King Alonso of Naples, who sent soldiers to arrest us so that Antonio could take my place. "

Miranda listened in astonishment.

"Antonio was afraid that the people of Milan would turn against him if they saw us harmed," Prospero continued, "so he sent us away on a ship. Once at sea, we were cruelly set adrift in a little boat without a sail. Luckily, we came ashore on this island, where I have done my best to care for you ever since."

Miranda was filled with pity for her father. "But why did you raise such a storm?" she asked.

"Alonso and my brother were aboard that ship," Prospero explained. "Now, by the use of my magic arts, our fortunes shall change. But there is no more time for questions." The wizard cast his hand across his daughter's eyes and she fell into an enchanted sleep.

Prospero took up his staff once more. "Ariel, sweet spirit," he called. In an instant he was surrounded by dancing lights and a merry-faced boy with shimmering wings fluttered before him. When Prospero arrived on the island he'd found Ariel imprisoned in a hollow tree by the witch Sycorax, who had died and left him there. Grateful to be rescued, Ariel now delighted in attending to Prospero's wishes.

THE TEMPEST

"All hail, master!" Ariel cried. He turned a somersault in the air. "I come to do your bidding; to fly, to swim, to dive into the fire or ride on the billowy clouds!"

Prospero smiled. "Did you take care of the ship as I asked?" he said.

"It's safely hidden in the bay, with the crew fast asleep below deck," replied Ariel, "and I made sure that everyone who leapt from the ship has come ashore unharmed."

Prospero was pleased. "Then bring me Alonso's son, Ferdinand," he said. Ariel made a bow, spun about and vanished.

Prospero turned to his cave at the foot of the cliff nearby. Grunts and groans echoed within, then out of the gloom shuffled Caliban; an ugly, scaly-skinned creature, half-man and half-monster. Caliban was the son of the witch Sycorax and had been left alone on the island when she died. Now, resentfully, he served Prospero. When he saw his hated master he scowled and cursed under his breath.

"I hear your wicked words, Caliban," said Prospero. "For that you will be punished tonight with cramps and stitches!"

"Why are you mean to me?" whined Caliban. "This island was all my own until you took it from me. When you first came you treated me kindly and I showed you where to find food and water. Now you treat me as a slave and torment me." Caliban clambered onto the rocks and pointed a finger at Prospero. "Toads, beetles and bats rain down on you!" he cried.

"You're nothing but a villain," said Prospero angrily. "I gave you a home in my own cave and taught you to speak but you repaid my kindness by trying to steal Miranda away." He raised his hand and Caliban cowered. "Get out of my sight and fetch the firewood, or I'll make your bones ache so much that wild beasts will tremble at the sound of your roar."

Afraid of the wizard's mighty power, Caliban scuttled away into the woods and obediently collected firewood. A short while later, he heard voices nearby. Caliban crept close. Alonso's jester and butler had also jumped from the storm-tossed ship and been cast up onto the island where, to their delight, they'd found a barrel of wine.

Caliban saw a chance for revenge on Prospero. He greeted the strangers, who were too

THE TEMPEST

drunk to be afraid of him. "Oh, great gods!" Caliban cried, bowing before them. "Save me, I beg you, for I am the slave of a wicked master. If you can get rid of him this island will be yours and I will serve you instead."

The jester nudged the butler and they both giggled. This is a fine adventure, they thought.

"I can lead you to the place where my master sleeps every afternoon," said Caliban cunningly. He waved a heavy club and grinned. "The rest is easy."

Wine had made the two men bold. They agreed to follow Caliban. "Lead on, monster," cried the butler. "We'll do as you say. I shall be King of this island and you and the jester shall both be Princes!"

Nobody noticed lights sparkling among the branches above as Ariel, sat in a tree, listened to every word.

Ariel flew away to fetch Ferdinand. He found him in a leafy glade, sitting with his head in his hands, full of sorrow at the loss of his father who he was sure must be drowned. Ariel made himself invisible and began to sing.

Ferdinand looked up. "This is the same voice that I followed as I swam for my life," he said. "And these are the strange, enchanting lights that led me to safety." He rose to his feet as if in a dream and followed Ariel through the wood.

When Prospero saw Ferdinand approach, he woke Miranda from her sleep. She gazed at the handsome young prince in wonder.

"Is this a spirit?" she asked, for she had never seen any man except her father.

"No, he eats and sleeps, just like us," Prospero assured her. "He was travelling on the ship and now searches for his lost companions."

Ariel's song ended and Ferdinand woke from his trance to see Miranda's beautiful face before him.

"I should have guessed that such heavenly music was playing for a goddess," he sighed, staring at her in amazement.

Miranda blushed. "I'm not a goddess," she said shyly.

Prospero saw that Miranda and Ferdinand had fallen in love at first sight. "They only have eyes for each other," he thought, with satisfaction. "My plan goes well."

Then Ariel told his master about Caliban's murderous plot.

"We must find a way to delay him," said Prospero, "for there is still more to be done to put things right here."

THE TEMPEST

On the other side of the island, Alonso and Antonio had been walking for hours looking for Ferdinand. Alonso feared that his son had drowned. "I'm sure some strange fish has made a meal of him," he sighed woefully. Tired and losing hope, they came to a woodland clearing. To their surprise a table stood before them, mysteriously set with a rich banquet of food.

"This island is a strange, enchanted place," said Alonso, warily. "If that banquet is real then I'll believe in unicorns!" The two hungry men held back afraid, but the delicious smell of the food became irresistible. However, as soon as they touched the dishes they were dazzled by a flash of light.

Ariel appeared as a huge bird of prey with a human head. He hovered over the food menacingly. Alonso and Antonio shrank away from his sharp talons.

"Why have you come to torment us?" they asked.

Ariel fixed them with a piercing stare. "You took what belonged to Duke Prospero," he cried. "You left him and his daughter to the mercy of the sea. Now Fate has robbed you of your son, Alonso, and brought you both to this desolate island to suffer your punishment."

Alonso and Antonio realised the terrible consequence of what they had done. "I should never have betrayed my brother's trust," said Antonio.

"We sent Prospero and Miranda away to die," sighed Alonso sorrowfully. They were both filled with shame.

Ariel opened his wings as if to swoop down upon them but with a clap of thunder he disappeared, the table vanished and they were left alone.

Unseen, Ariel flew off to find Caliban, who was leading his new friends through the wood towards Prospero's cave. "This task will be more entertaining," Ariel said to himself. He called

THE TEMPEST

up the dark spirits of the island who came bounding out of the shadows as huge red-eyed hunting dogs.

Caliban and his drunken friends stopped in their tracks. They stared in horror at the terrifying hounds, then turned on their heels and ran for their lives, shrieking as they crashed through the brambles and thorns.

Prospero appeared at Ariel's side. "You've served me well, sweet Ariel," he said. "Now my enemies are all at my mercy."

"Alonso and Antonio are full of regret for what they did to you," Ariel assured him.

"Then that is all I wish," said Prospero. "Bring them to me now. Although I have good reason for revenge, it is better to forgive."

Prospero returned to the beach. There, he drew a circle in the sand with his staff. Alonso and Antonio stepped out of the trees into the circle. At first they didn't recognise Prospero but when he removed his magic cloak they gasped to see the old Duke, who they thought had died at sea long ago. Alonso and Antonio sank to their knees and begged forgiveness for their treacherous acts. Seeing they were truly sorry, Prospero forgave them both.

"Your home and title shall be restored to you," promised Alonso. "But sadly, I can never regain the son I lost in the storm."

Prospero nodded thoughtfully. "I lost my daughter in the storm, too," he said.

Alonso wept with pity for them both. "I'd give my life to take my son's place sleeping on the muddy seabed," he said. "If only our children could be alive as King and Queen of Naples."

"Let's rest awhile," suggested Prospero, and he led the way to his cave.

To Alonso's astonishment, when they came to the cave, they found Ferdinand and Miranda, very much alive and in love. Alonso and his son were joyfully reunited. Then Prospero laid down his magic staff, for all was right with the world once more.

A shower of lights danced and sparkled in the sunlight. "Ariel, my tricksy spirit!" Prospero greeted him with thanks. "My enemies are now my friends and our children, joined in love, shall build a better world together. Gather the castaways, go wake the crew and bring us the ship. I release you from my service to fly free as the sea spray."

And so it was time for everyone to leave the magical world of spirits and sail home.

Only Caliban remained, happy at last to be King of his island once more.

"If music be the food of love, play on."

TWELFTH NIGHT

CAST OF CHARACTERS

Viola / Cesario
Sebastian's sister disguised
as Duke Orsino's page

Sebastian
Viola's twin brother,
lost at sea

TWELFTH
NIGHT

Olivia
A Countess,
in mourning

Sir Toby Belch
Olivia's uncle,
a merry old man

Orsino
Duke of Illyria,
in love with Olivia

Maria
Olivia's maid

Malvolio
Olivia's steward

Sir Andrew
Friend of Sir Toby's

TWELFTH NIGHT

TWELFTH NIGHT

Duke Orsino lived by the rocky coast of Illyria. Every day he gazed out at the sparkling sapphire sea and sighed for love of the beautiful Countess Olivia. Orsino desperately longed to marry her, but Olivia's brother had recently died and she'd vowed to live in mourning for seven years. To the Duke's dismay, she refused to see him, or even read his love letters.

Nevertheless, Orsino wouldn't be put off. He enjoyed being in love, even if his feelings were rejected. Love filled him with romantic dreams and poetry. "If music is the food of love, play on!" he told his minstrels. Happy or sad, the Duke loved to be in love.

"Olivia shows deep affection for her brother," he said to his new page, Cesario, one day. "Imagine how much she'll love me when I make her my wife."

Cesario gazed at the Duke's handsome face and nodded silently.

Little did the Duke know that he wasn't the only one in love; Cesario was really a young woman called Viola, who had disguised herself to work at the Duke's house and had fallen in love with him. Three months earlier, Viola had been on a voyage with her twin brother, Sebastian, when their ship was wrecked in a storm. Viola clung to the broken mast and was washed up on the shore near the Duke's house, but sadly her brother couldn't be found and she feared he had drowned. However, Viola was not the sort of girl to sit and weep over her misfortune for long. Among the wreckage she discovered a chest of clothes and decided it would be easier to get by in the world alone if she pretended to be a man. It was a disguise that not only concealed her identity but, before long, also hid her secret love for Orsino.

Orsino was pleased with the new page, who had soon become his favourite. "You have such a sweet face and a gentle voice, Cesario," he said one day, "I'm sure Olivia couldn't turn you away. Go to her house and tell her how much I long to have her for my wife. Refuse to leave until she lets you speak."

Viola's heart sank. "What a task," she sighed to herself as she set off along the cliff path. "I must win a wife for the man I love myself!"

At the gate of Olivia's house, Viola was met by Malvolio, the steward who ran her household.

TWELFTH NIGHT

"You're wasting your time," Malvolio said when he heard her request. "My Mistress refuses to receive any young men."

"Well, I refuse to leave without speaking to her," replied Viola stubbornly. Exasperated, Malvolio went to tell Olivia. The Countess was intrigued by this determined visitor and, having nothing better to do, agreed to see him.

Viola greeted Olivia with praise. "Most radiant, exquisite and unmatchable beauty," she began, "my master adores you, with groans that thunder love and sighs of fire."

Olivia felt her cheeks blush at the sight of the striking young man before her, who spoke with such passion. The more Olivia listened to Viola's flattering words, the more she forgot her objection to love. But it was the messenger who stirred her heart, not the master!

"Although the Duke is a fine and noble man, I cannot love him," Olivia told Viola. "Give your master this reply, Cesario, but return at once to tell me how he takes the news."

Viola knew that the Duke would be disappointed. "I did my best," she thought to herself. "If only I could take Olivia's place in Orsino's heart."

As Viola walked away from the house, Malvolio called her back. He handed her a gold ring. "It seems you left this with my mistress," he said, "but she wishes you to have it." And with a disapproving frown he turned and shut the door.

Viola was puzzled. "I didn't bring a ring, why would Olivia wish me to have one?" With shock she realised that it must be a love token. "Oh dear, the Countess would do better to love a dream," Viola sighed. "I never guessed this disguise would cause so much trouble. Olivia has fallen in love with me, but I love the Duke and he only has eyes for Olivia. This knot is too hard for me to untangle!"

Although Olivia had made a vow to mourn for seven years her house was far from quiet, for it was also home to her uncle, Sir Toby Belch, a merry old man who loved feasting, drinking and having fun. Sir Toby was often joined by his rich, dim-witted friend, Sir Andrew, who he hoped would one day marry Olivia.

That evening, Sir Toby and Sir Andrew made so much noise with their rowdy laughter that Malvolio appeared in his nightclothes. "You make this place sound like an ale-house!" he complained. "If you don't stop this bad behaviour then my Lady will turn you out."

When Malvolio had gone back to bed, Sir Toby and Sir Andrew decided to get their own back by having some fun at his expense. Olivia's maid, Maria, offered to help.

"Malvolio thinks he is so crammed with excellence that everyone admires him," Maria said, "but that's his weakness. Tomorrow, I'll write a letter in Lady Olivia's handwriting that will make Malvolio believe she loves him. All you have to do is hide and watch how he makes a fool of himself."

"Excellent!" said Sir Toby and Sir Andrew and they chuckled with anticipation.

Next day, as Malvolio was walking through the garden imagining what a fine Count he would make, he found a letter in what looked like Olivia's handwriting, lying on the path. He didn't notice Sir Toby, Sir Andrew and Maria watching from behind a bush.

The letter fell open in his hand. "To my secret love," he read. "Although I am above you, do not fear greatness. Some are born great, some achieve greatness, and some have greatness thrust upon them. Forget your humble position and act as my equal. If you love me, show me with a smile and wear the yellow stockings I admire."

Malvolio gazed at the letter in a daze. "The stars be praised. Lady Olivia loves me!" he cried. "I will do everything she asks." He hurried off at once to find his yellow stockings.

Sir Toby and Sir Andrew exploded with laughter.

"Lady Olivia loathes those yellow stockings," giggled Maria. "And she won't like Malvolio's creepy smile either. Ever since the Duke's messenger came here she's been all out of sorts."

"Here's the fellow again!" said Sir Toby. "Look! Let's hide to see what message he brings this time."

Viola walked up the path, her heart heavy to see Olivia come out to meet her. As Viola had expected, Duke Orsino wouldn't accept Olivia's rejection. He had sent her back with a gift of a jewelled brooch, which she now gave to Olivia.

"I wish the Duke's thoughts were empty, rather than filled with me," said Olivia with a sigh. She took Viola's hand. "Won't you wear the ring I sent, Cesario? You are the one I love."

Sir Toby and Sir Andrew were astonished at what they heard. They slipped away, back to the house.

"The Countess shows this page more affection than she's ever shown me!" exclaimed Sir Andrew.

"No, no," replied Sir Toby, seeing a chance for mischief. "Olivia must have noticed we were listening. She's trying to stir you up to fight for her! You must impress her by challenging that

TWELFTH
NIGHT

young page to a duel." Fired with jealousy, Sir Andrew agreed and went off to fetch his sword.

Sir Toby grinned to himself. "That hopeless fool hasn't got a clue about duelling," he thought, "and the page is obviously as gentle as a lamb. I'm sure they couldn't harm each other if they tried but it'll be fun to watch!"

Meanwhile, Viola wished that she didn't have to deceive poor love-struck Olivia but she couldn't reveal the truth. "I'm not what I seem, my lady," she said gently. "No woman will ever be mistress of my heart." And with that she tugged her hand free and hurried away through the garden.

Olivia sat in the orchard feeling miserable. "What can I do to make Cesario change his mind?" she wondered. Her thoughts were disturbed by the maid, Maria, who came running up with a worried look.

"I've come to warn you about Malvolio, my lady," she said. "He's acting very strange."

At that moment Malvolio came strutting down the path, wearing yellow stockings and a creepy smile.

"Why do you smile like that, Malvolio?" asked Olivia.

"To please my sweetheart," said Malvolio, grinning from ear to ear. He plucked a rose and offered it to Olivia. "See, it's yellow to match the stockings she adores." Then to Olivia's amazement he blew her a kiss.

"How dare you be so bold with my lady," said Maria, trying hard not to laugh.

"Some of us will soon have greatness thrust upon them," Malvolio replied grandly and he

TWELFTH
NIGHT

pranced before them in his yellow stockings like a frolicking jester.

Olivia stared in bewilderment. "I do believe Malvolio has completely lost his senses, Maria," she said. "Take him away and have the doctor put him to bed for a week!"

While Malvolio was acting out this strange pantomime, Viola left Olivia's house, thinking that she'd had a narrow escape. But Sir Andrew, egged on by Sir Toby, was waiting for her in the street.

"I challenge you to a duel, knave!" Sir Andrew cried and he drew his sword.

Viola was terrified. "I've done nothing wrong," she stuttered. "Please let me pass."

At that moment, a rough-looking sailor appeared. "If you have a problem with this gentleman then you can fight me," he growled at Sir Andrew and he began rolling up his sleeves right there and then.

Sir Andrew trembled like a jelly. He hurriedly sheathed his sword, muttered something about a mistake and turned tail, with Sir Toby hurrying after him.

Viola breathed a sigh of relief. "How can I thank you for your help?" she asked the sailor.

"Thank me?" The sailor looked surprised. "We look after each other, my friend."

At that moment, an officer of the law marched up. "I'm arresting you for stealing from Duke Orsino's ship," he announced.

The sailor looked worriedly at Viola. "I can pay my way out of this if you give me back my purse," he said.

"But I don't have your purse," replied Viola, wishing things would stop being so confusing.

"Don't play games," the sailor pleaded. He turned to the officer. "I saved this man from drowning," he said. "Now he pretends that he doesn't have the purse I lent him!"

But the officer just shrugged and tied the man's hands. As he was led away, the sailor looked back and cried, "Shame on you, Sebastian!"

"Sebastian?" Viola's heart leapt. She didn't dare believe her ears. Had this man mistaken Viola for her twin brother? If so, then Sebastian must be alive. But where was he?

As it happened, Sebastian wasn't far away. Not long after Viola had left Olivia's house, he walked by and Olivia saw him from her window. Mistaking him for Cesario, she thought the page had decided to return to her and rushed out to greet him.

"Oh, I knew you'd come," she cried and she flung her arms around him.

Sebastian was completely baffled but he wasn't one to resist a beautiful woman. "Either I'm mad or this is a dream," he thought with amusement. "But if so, let me sleep on!" Determined not to let her love escape again, Olivia led Sebastian into the house and he willingly followed.

Next day, the Duke himself came to see Olivia, with Viola at his side. Olivia stared at Viola with a puzzled look.

"Good lady, heaven walks on earth!" said the Duke with a bow.

"That's a strange thing to say in front of my husband," replied Olivia.

"Husband?" The Duke was taken aback.

TWELFTH NIGHT

"Yes, tell him, Cesario," said Olivia. "We were married this morning. But why are you back at the Duke's side? Orsino isn't your master any more."

"Yes he is," said Viola. "He's the master I love more than life itself. More than I shall ever love a wife."

Everyone was feeling very confused, when suddenly Sebastian walked into the room with a radiant smile and Olivia's wedding ring on his finger.

Viola and Sebastian stared at each other in amazement. "I never had a brother, Sir," said Sebastian, "but surely we must be family?"

Viola laughed. To everyone's astonishment, she pulled off her page's cap and down tumbled her long red hair, as red as her dearest brother's beard.

There was never a happier reunion and so much explaining to do. When everyone's stories had been told several times, and all was finally understood, the Duke graciously gave the happy couple his blessing and the Countess gave her new sister, Viola, a dress to wear for the wedding celebrations.

That night, the house was filled with laughter and music. Sir Toby and Sir Andrew enjoyed the feast and Malvolio, still blushing from his embarrassment, kept the candles burning late.

Orsino gazed with admiration at his page, now transformed into a beautiful young woman. "Do you really love me more than life itself, Viola?" he asked. Viola didn't need to say a word. Her sparkling eyes told him of the loving feelings she'd had to hide for so long.

Then Orsino smiled and offered her his hand. "If music be the food of love," he said, "let the minstrels play on!"

"O, beware, my lord, of jealousy:
It is the green-eyed monster which doth mock
The meat it feeds on."

OTHELLO

CAST OF CHARACTERS

Othello
A general of the
Venetian army

Desdemona
A noblewoman,
wife of Othello

OTHELLO

Iago
Othello's most
trusted attendant

Cassio
Othello's lieutenant,
friend of Desdemona

Roderigo
A young soldier,
in love with Desdemona

OTHELLO

Othello was an exceptional man. As a Moor, it was unusual to have a powerful position in Venice, but his courage, honesty and good judgement had earned him promotion to a general and he was much respected by the Duke of Venice himself. His stories of travel and adventure on his campaigns had captured the heart of a nobleman's daughter, called Desdemona. She loved Othello for the dangers he'd overcome and he grew to love her gentle, caring nature. However, Desdemona knew that her father wouldn't approve of her marrying someone of a different race, so she and Othello were married in secret.

When Desdemona's father heard about the marriage he was furious. He disowned his daughter completely. "Watch her closely," he warned Othello. "If she can deceive her father, one day she may deceive you too!"

Othello dismissed his words with scorn. "Desdemona's heart is pure," he insisted. "I would trust my life to her honesty."

Soon after the wedding, Othello set sail from Venice to become the Governor of the island of Cyprus and Desdemona went with him.

Among the men who accompanied them were Othello's trusted attendant, Iago, and a young soldier called Roderigo, who had long been secretly in love with Desdemona. Roderigo was feeling full of despair at Desdemona's marriage.

"To live now is torment," he moaned to Iago as they sailed towards Cyprus. "I might as well drown myself!"

"Don't give up," said Iago. "Desdemona will soon lose interest in Othello's exotic looks. Before long she'll want a fine Venetian man like yourself. Trust me, when she does I'll help you win her."

"Why would you help me?" asked Roderigo.

Iago scowled. "I hate Othello," he said. "We shouldn't have to take orders from a Moor and he promoted Cassio to be his lieutenant instead of me. If I help you steal Othello's wife I shall have my revenge."

Later, alone in his cabin Iago plotted secretly against Othello. "Maybe there's a way to punish him and get rid of Cassio too," he thought to himself. "Cassio and Desdemona are friends. If I trick Othello into believing that they love each other, then suspicion and jealousy will do my work." Iago smiled wickedly. "Othello foolishly believes that all men are as honest as they seem. He'll be led to his fate as easily as an ass!"

OTHELLO

When the Venetian ships arrived in Cyprus, Iago began at once to put his plan into action. That evening, he persuaded Cassio, who was in charge of the watchmen, to share a drink with him. Cassio protested that he wasn't a drinking man, but Iago lied that the wine was very weak. Before long, all the watchmen were singing and Cassio was stumbling drunkenly on his feet. Iago cleverly stirred up trouble between them. In the heat of the moment swords were drawn and rowdy shouts echoed through the garrison.

Othello appeared, angry at the disturbance. When he discovered that Cassio was drunk in charge of the watch he was deeply disappointed.

"Cassio, I love you as my friend," he said sternly, "but you can no longer be my officer."

Cassio was devastated. As soon as Othello left, cunning Iago comforted him.

"Don't worry, Cassio, this isn't a serious offence," said Iago. "Visit Desdemona tomorrow and ask her to plead with Othello to change his mind. He is so in love with her, he'll do anything she asks."

Cassio was grateful for Iago's support. "You advise me well, honest friend," he said. "I'll ask for Desdemona's help in the morning."

That night, Iago laughed at how easily Cassio was fooled. "Tomorrow I'll pour poisonous words into Othello's ears to make him believe that Cassio and his wife love each other. Desdemona will have no idea that when she pleads for mercy on Cassio's behalf she'll be making a net to trap them all!"

Next morning, Iago made sure that Othello was out of the way so that Cassio could speak to Desdemona. When she heard about Cassio's punishment she took pity on him at once and promised to help him. "I know that you love Othello," she said. "Don't worry, he'll have no peace from me until you are forgiven."

At that moment, Othello and Iago returned. "Here comes my husband," said Desdemona. "Stay and hear me talk to him." But Cassio hadn't slept all night and didn't want Othello to see him in such a bad way. He thanked Desdemona and hurried away.

"Was that Cassio with my wife?" Othello asked Iago.

"Surely not," said Iago slyly. "Why would Cassio sneak away with such a guilty look when he saw you coming?"

Desdemona wasted no time in talking to Othello about Cassio. "He's truly sorry," she said. "If I have any grace or power to move you, show him your forgiveness, my lord."

"Anything for you," said Othello, wishing only to please her. "Cassio may speak to me later." Satisfied with this, Desdemona left him.

"Fair lady," sighed Othello, gazing after her. "How I love her. If ever my love ends the world will fall into chaos."

"I didn't realise that Cassio was your wife's friend," said Iago casually.

"Yes," replied Othello. "He often visited her on my behalf before we were married."

"Indeed!" Iago exclaimed. "You trusted them alone together?"

Othello wondered why Iago was surprised at this. "Don't you think he's trustworthy?"

Iago looked thoughtful for a moment. "Men should be what they seem," he answered, "and Cassio seems honest."

"Seems honest?" Othello sensed that Iago was hiding something. "Tell me what you mean."

"It's my duty to serve you, my lord," replied Iago, "but you cannot command me to speak my thoughts."

As Iago intended, Othello began to suspect that he knew something about Cassio and Desdemona that he wasn't saying. But Othello wouldn't be led to doubt his wife so easily.

"I may have faults but Desdemona chose me with her eyes open, and she loves me. I won't doubt her without evidence."

"I only speak out of love for you, my lord," said Iago with a bow. "Just remember, she deceived her father when she married you."

All that day, Othello wrestled with the suspicion Iago had planted in his mind. "I would rather be a toad living in a dungeon than share the one I love with another man," he thought wretchedly. "Is it possible that Desdemona regrets marrying an older man, or longs for more refined, courtly manners than those of a soldier like me?"

At supper time, when Desdemona came to tell Othello that their dinner guests had arrived, she noticed his pained expression. "Are you ill, my love?" she asked.

Othello muttered that he had a headache. Desdemona fetched a handkerchief to cool his brow but he pushed it away. "That's too small to do any good," he said. "Let's not keep our

OTHELLO

guests waiting."

While they were at dinner, Iago's wife Emilia, who was Desdemona's maid, found the little handkerchief on the floor. "This is the first gift Othello gave to my mistress," she remembered with a smile. "Desdemona promised to keep it forever."

At that moment, Iago came into the room and saw the handkerchief in Emilia's hand. Quick as a flash, he snatched it from her.

"I want this to play a trick on someone," he told his wife. The handkerchief was just the evidence he needed to destroy Cassio and get his revenge on Othello.

All through dinner, Othello was tormented by thoughts of Desdemona and Cassio together. Next day, he told Iago that he wanted proof. "If you've lied, I'll punish you so harshly that you'll wish you'd been born a dog!" he warned.

OTHELLO

Iago was ready with more poisonous words for Othello's ears. He told him that he'd heard Cassio talk about Desdemona in his sleep and seen him wipe his beard with her favourite handkerchief. Iago didn't mention that he'd put the handkerchief in Cassio's room himself.

Othello was outraged. "Betrayed with my own love token!" he cried. "And now Desdemona dares to plead on Cassio's behalf for my forgiveness!" Anger burned in his heart.

Iago turned away with secret satisfaction.

The following day, Othello watched Desdemona closely. He asked to borrow the handkerchief that he'd given her but, as he expected, she didn't have it.

"Is it lost?" he asked.

"No, my lord," said Desdemona.

"Then where is it?" said Othello.

"It's not lost, but what if it were?" answered Desdemona.

"If it's not lost, bring it here," Othello demanded angrily. "Let me see it."

Desdemona was alarmed by Othello's fierce mood. "I came to ask you again about Cassio – is this a trick to distract me?" she said. "Please, my lord, send for him and take him back into your service."

The mention of Cassio made Othello furious and he stormed out of the room.

Next morning, Iago offered Othello further proof of Desdemona's betrayal. He arranged to meet Cassio in the town square and suggested that Othello watch them from the window of the tavern. "I'll ask Cassio about his meetings with Desdemona," said Iago. "Watch his reaction. Although you won't hear his words, you'll see his guilt for yourself."

However, when Cassio arrived, instead of asking him about Desdemona, Iago asked about a girl from the tavern called Bianca. Othello watched Cassio smile.

"Bianca's easily pleased," said Cassio. "When I gave her a handkerchief I found she smothered me with kisses!"

"Then you should marry her," suggested Iago.

"Marry her?" Cassio laughed. "She's fine company for an evening but I don't love her!"

At that moment, Bianca appeared from the tavern door, having heard Cassio's words. She flung Desdemona's handkerchief at him.

"My handkerchief!" cried Othello, watching from the window.

"You can keep your present," Bianca sobbed and she ran away. Cassio followed after her.

Iago beckoned to Othello. "Did you witness how Cassio laughed and smiled when I asked about Desdemona?" he said artfully. "And did you see the handkerchief?"

"My heart is turned to stone," uttered Othello. "Death is the only punishment for Cassio. You shall be my lieutenant now, Iago. Fetch me some poison, Desdemona has brought dishonour upon us both and must die for it too."

"Better to strangle her in bed," whispered Iago. "That is the place she shared with Cassio."

That evening, Roderigo came to Iago's room to complain that he'd had no help in his quest to win Desdemona. Iago saw a chance for Roderigo to do his dirty work.

"Desdemona is already bored with Othello," Iago told him. "Cassio is your rival now. Help me kill him tonight and then the path will be clear for you." Reluctantly, Roderigo agreed.

OTHELLO

Together, they ambushed Cassio in a dark alleyway, but Roderigo's blow only delivered a wound. Disturbed by passers by, Iago protected himself by plunging his knife into Roderigo's back and fled, unseen.

Meanwhile, Othello came to Desdemona's bedchamber and found her sleeping peacefully. He gazed at her beautiful face, seeming so innocent in the lantern light. Hot tears rolled down his cheeks.

"Put out the light and then put out the light," he murmured, trembling at the deed before him. "If I quench the lantern flame I can restore it but if I put out the light of your life, fair Desdemona, it cannot be rekindled."

He kissed her and she woke.

"Have you said your prayers?" whispered Othello.

"Yes, my lord," replied Desdemona.

"Then you are ready to die for your sins."

Desdemona gasped. "Why do you talk of killing?"

"I know you have been unfaithful with Cassio," said Othello. "I saw the proof of the handkerchief you gave him."

"It's not true!" Desdemona cried. "Bring Cassio here and he'll tell you so."

"Iago has already seen to his punishment," said Othello.

Desdemona cried out in terror. She saw that the truth couldn't help her. "Banish me, my lord, if I can't prove my innocence, don't kill me," she pleaded.

But Othello was possessed. His justice was beyond mercy. He seized a pillow and smothered Desdemona until she lay lifeless.

Emilia heard the noise and hurried into the room.

Othello threw the pillow to the floor. "My wife was unfaithful with Cassio," he told her. "It was only your honest husband who told me the truth."

Emilia stared in disbelief. "You are wrong, my lord," she gasped. "My mistress was always faithful." She ran to the door and shouted "Murder!"

Iago and the guards came running.

Emilia confronted her husband. "Tell Othello that you lied about my mistress," she demanded.

Iago gripped the hilt of his sword. "I only said what I thought," he replied.

"And I saw the proof," said Othello. "Cassio had Desdemona's handkerchief, my first token of love."

Emilia stared with horror at her husband. "But Iago took that handkerchief from me," she cried. "He said he wanted to play a trick on someone. He must have given it to Cassio himself!"

The truth struck Othello like a thunderbolt. He'd been tricked into murdering his innocent wife. "Villain!" he roared. But before Othello could reach for his weapon, Iago thrust his sword into Emilia's heart and ran from the room, chased by the guards.

Othello sank to his knees with grief at what he'd done. "Oh, Desdemona, my life, my love!" he cried. "How could I believe a devil and doubt your pure heart? I loved not wisely, but too well. Nothing I did was for hate, only for honour." With one last look at her angelic face Othello stabbed himself and fell into her arms, their lips meeting in a final kiss.

OTHELLO

*"All the world's a stage,
And all the men and women merely players."*

AS YOU
LIKE
IT

CAST OF CHARACTERS

Rosalind
A noblewoman,
Duke Senior's daughter

Celia
Duke Frederick's
daughter; Rosalind's
cousin

Oliver
First son of Sir Rowland
de Bois; Orlando's
brother

AS YOU
LIKE IT

Orlando
Second son of Sir
Rowland de Bois;
Oliver's brother

Charles
Duke Frederick's prize
fighter

Duke Senior
Duke Frederick's
brother, banished to the
Forest of Arden

AS YOU LIKE IT

When Sir Rowland de Bois died, his eldest son Oliver inherited all his wealth. Oliver had promised Sir Rowland that he'd take good care of his younger brother, Orlando, but it was a promise that he didn't keep for long. Jealous of Orlando's good looks and confident nature, Oliver made his brother eat with the servants, refused to let him go to school and let him have very little money.

One day, Orlando decided to disguise his noble birth and take part in a wrestling match which offered valuable prize money. The champion was Duke Frederick's prize fighter, Charles. Orlando was about to enter the ring when two young ladies pushed through the crowd. One of them was Celia, Duke Frederick's daughter and the other was her cousin, Rosalind.

"Sir," said Celia, "please change your mind, there is little chance of winning. Three opponents have already been carried off with broken ribs today!"

"Yes, save yourself," pleaded Rosalind, who couldn't help but stare at Orlando's handsome face.

Orlando was touched by their concern and thanked them but he wouldn't change his mind. "Your kind wishes will strengthen me in the fight," he assured them, "for there is nobody else in the world who cares if I live or die."

His brave, sad words stirred Rosalind's heart. "Then I give you what little strength I have myself," she said earnestly. And the girls took their places to watch the match.

The fight began. Charles was as strong as an ox but Orlando was nimble and quick. He ducked and dived, outwitting the older man until he saw his chance, gripped Charles and threw him to the ground with a thud. The champion was beaten. The crowd cheered but Orlando only had eyes for Rosalind.

Duke Frederick presented Orlando with his prize money. "You are a brave youth," he said.

"Who is your father?"

"My father is dead," replied Orlando. "I am the youngest son of Sir Rowland de Bois."

The Duke's smile vanished. "Then you are the son of my enemy," he said bitterly. Without another word, he and his attendants left.

On an impulse Rosalind undid the chain around her neck and gave it to Orlando.

"You've won over more than your enemy today, Sir," she said boldly. "Please, wear this and remember me."

As she walked away, Orlando asked a courtier who she was.

"That's Rosalind," said the courtier. "Her father, Duke Senior, is Duke Frederick's brother. Long ago, Duke Frederick banished him to the forest but Rosalind was allowed to remain as a companion for Duke Frederick's daughter, Celia. The girls have grown up as sisters but recently the Duke has noticed that Rosalind gets more attention than Celia. Duke Frederick is a wicked man, Sir. I fear it won't be long before he finds an excuse to banish Rosalind, just like her father."

"Oh, heavenly Rosalind!" sighed Orlando. "Life has also been unfair to her. I know we are meant for each other." He kissed the chain she'd given him and hung it next to his heart. With a nod of thanks to the courtier he walked away, smiling happily.

That afternoon, Rosalind talked so much about brave, handsome Orlando that Celia couldn't resist teasing her. But their high spirits were interrupted when the Duke suddenly burst into their room. To Rosalind's horror he accused her of being disloyal and plotting with

Orlando against him. "I saw you together at the wrestling match," he said with contempt. "Your fathers were friends and both my enemies."

"I've done nothing wrong," protested Rosalind but the Duke refused to listen.

"You are a traitor, just like your father," he told her. "I have raised you as my own child but I can no longer trust you. I banish you from court."

"Rosalind's as innocent as I am," Celia cried. "If you send her away then I'll go too!" However, the Duke's mind was made up and nothing would change it. "You must be gone tomorrow," he insisted and he stormed out of the room.

"What shall we do?" cried Rosalind.

"Let's go to the Forest of Arden and search for your father," suggested Celia.

Rosalind hugged her cousin. "Thank you, loyal friend," she said, "that's a perfect plan."

Early next morning, the girls disguised themselves. Celia dressed as a shepherdess and Rosalind tucked her long hair into a hat and dressed herself as a man. "I shall wear a sword to frighten away any trouble!" she said. Then Celia gathered her money and jewels and they set off for the forest, full of thoughts of adventure.

Duke Frederick was furious when he learnt that Celia had left with Rosalind. He sent for her maid, who'd heard the girls talk about Orlando the day before. "So I was right!" said the Duke. He summoned Orlando's brother, Oliver.

"Bring me Orlando, dead or alive," the Duke demanded. "If you fail, I shall confiscate everything you own."

Oliver didn't need any persuading. "Here's an opportunity to get rid of Orlando and keep all Father's wealth for myself," he thought, so he agreed to do as the Duke asked.

Meanwhile, Celia and Rosalind arrived at the forest, where they soon found a little cottage for sale and set up a new home together. They were unaware that Orlando had also come to the forest. He wandered among the leafy glades until, tired and hungry, he came to the camp where Duke Senior and his men were living.

Duke Senior recognised Orlando at once as the son of his old friend and welcomed him into their forest home. "It's a care-free life here under the greenwood trees," he told Orlando with a beaming smile. "You must join us. Nature gives us all we need!"

Orlando soon settled into his new life but although he had a soft mossy bed and good company he was not content. All day long he yearned for Rosalind. As he was unable to tell her of his feelings, Orlando wrote love poems to her and pinned them on the trees.

One morning, when Rosalind and Celia were out picking berries they found one of the poems, full of romantic declarations of love. "Who could this secret writer be?" wondered Rosalind. Just then, they heard somebody talking nearby. To their surprise they saw Orlando sitting with a quill pen and a bottle of ink, murmuring rhymes to himself. Rosalind was filled with joy. "Let's see if Orlando really does love me," she whispered to Celia with a wink. Hoping that he wouldn't see through her disguise she boldly strolled over to him.

"Sir," she said, "do you know who is littering the forest with all this romantic nonsense?"

Orlando jumped to his feet. "Those are my poems," he said, looking offended. "And it's not nonsense, I'm in love with a wonderful girl."

Rosalind eyed him up and down. "Hmmm. You don't look like somebody in love to me," she scoffed. "If you were in love you'd look wretched and miserable. Love is nothing more than a disease. Why, I cured a man of it once."

Orlando was curious. "How did you do that?" he asked.

80

"By giving him a good dose of it," said Rosalind. "You see, I told him to imagine that I was his love. First I encouraged him, then I rejected him. One moment I was gentle, then cruel, adoring, suspicious, full of smiles, then floods of tears. It wasn't long before he'd had enough of love's madness and was completely cured!"

Orlando laughed. "Well, you could never cure me," he said.

"Let me try," replied Rosalind mischievously. "I live in a cottage along the path with my sister. If you visit me and pretend that I'm your Rosalind I promise I'll cure you of love forever!"

"All right," said Orlando, amused to take up the challenge. "You'll soon see how strong my love is, young fellow."

Next day, Rosalind waited eagerly for Orlando but he didn't arrive. At last, an hour late, he appeared.

She greeted him with a scolding. "This is no way to treat the girl you love!" she said crossly.

"Forgive me, dearest Rosalind," said Orlando, playing his part.

"Well, you can make it up to me by telling me how much you care," said Rosalind playfully and she made a place for him to sit beside her. "Talk to me in words of love."

Orlando gazed deep into her eyes. He praised her with adoring words and poured out his heart. "I vow to love you for ever and a day," he said solemnly, taking her hand. "Will my Rosalind do the same?"

At the touch of his hand, Rosalind melted. She felt as if Orlando was looking straight into her heart. "Your Rosalind will do the same as I do," she answered.

For a moment it seemed as if time stood still. Neither of them moved or spoke. Then, breaking the spell, Orlando jumped to his feet and reached for his hat. "I must leave you now for a while," he said as it was time to eat at the camp, "but I promise to return at two o'clock."

As soon as Orlando had gone, Rosalind ran into the kitchen and flung her arms around Celia. "Oh cousin, if only you knew how much I love him!" she cried. "Every minute will be an hour until he returns."

However, when two o'clock came there was no sign of Orlando. Three o'clock went by and still he didn't appear. Rosalind paced up and down sighing so much that Celia took her out for a walk.

AS YOU LIKE IT

They hadn't gone far when Orlando's brother Oliver came along the path, clutching a blood-stained handkerchief.

"I'm looking for the young man who answers to the name of Rosalind," he said. "I bring a message from my brother, Orlando."

"This is Rosalind," said Celia, taking an instant fancy to the tall, dashing stranger.

"What's your message?" asked Rosalind. "Where is Orlando?"

Oliver told them that he'd been searching for Orlando in the forest for several days. "A few hours ago, while I was resting, a lioness appeared and was about to pounce on me when Orlando walked by. I'm ashamed to say that I've been a bad brother to him since our father died and have treated him unkindly, but without thinking of this or his own safety, Orlando fought off the lioness and saved my life. To my joy, we are now happily reconciled."

"Then whose blood is on the handkerchief?" asked Celia.

"Orlando was wounded," said Oliver. "He asked me to bring this handkerchief to prove why he wasn't able to keep his promise to return."

At the thought of Orlando's wounds Rosalind suddenly felt faint. Oliver offered to accompany them home and Celia eagerly agreed.

While Rosalind rested, Celia and Oliver enjoyed each other's company. By the end of the afternoon, as if the forest had cast a spell upon them both, they had fallen deeply in love.

When Rosalind awoke she was amazed to hear that Celia and Oliver had decided to marry.

"Be happy for us, cousin," said Celia.

Rosalind saw their joy and was delighted. Oliver explained that they wished to wed the very next day at Duke Senior's camp, where he had taken Orlando.

"Then tell your brother that I won't try and cure him any longer," said Rosalind. "I'll bring his love to him and there shall be two weddings in the forest tomorrow!"

Next morning, when Celia and Rosalind walked into Duke Senior's camp dressed in their own clothes there was great surprise and celebration. Oliver marvelled at the transformation of his shepherdess and Orlando felt his heart would burst with laughter when he heard of Rosalind's deception.

Duke Senior welcomed his long-lost daughter and his niece with great rejoicing. "I am overwhelmed with happiness!" he exclaimed.

However, their reunion was interrupted by a messenger who arrived with unexpected news. "Two days ago, Duke Frederick gathered an army to hunt down his enemies" he told Duke Senior. "But as he entered the forest he met a priest who made him see the wickedness of his ways. Now your brother has decided to join a monastery and leave all his land and wealth to you."

Everyone cheered. "Well, that's good news indeed," said Duke Senior. "But it matters not today. For all the wealth in the world cannot better this wonderful wedding celebration, here among the greenwood trees, the wild roses and the sweet songbirds of the forest."

AS YOU
LIKE IT

"Men at some time are masters of their fates.
The fault, dear Brutus, is not in our stars
But in ourselves, that we are underlings."

JULIUS
CAESAR

CAST OF CHARACTERS

Julius Caesar
A Roman general
and senator

Casca
Fellow conspirator
against Caesar

Brutus
A supporter of the
Republic

Marc Antony
Friend of Caesar

Cassius
A Roman general,
lead conspirator
against Caesar

Trebonius
Fellow conspirator
against Caesar

Octavius
Caesar's nephew and heir

JULIUS
CAESAR

JULIUS CAESAR

"Caesar! Caesar! Caesar!"

The people of Rome were gathered in the streets to honour their great general, Julius Caesar, who had returned from leading his army to victory. The excited crowd cheered as he rode proudly through the city, followed by a procession of noble senators.

Suddenly an old man stepped forward and waved his arms to halt the procession. Everyone fell silent and stared.

The old man pointed at Caesar with an expression full of doom. "Beware the Ides of March!" he cried.

"What are the Ides of March?" whispered a boy in the crowd.

"The fifteenth day of the month, which is tomorrow," his father replied. "That man is a soothsayer who foretells the future."

Caesar's stony face didn't flinch. He wasn't going to let an old man's warning spoil his triumphant day. "Pass on," he commanded and the soothsayer was pushed aside.

Watching nearby were two senators, Brutus and Cassius, who had been friends since childhood. "Listen to the crowd," said Brutus as people cheered once more. "They treat Caesar as if he were their king."

"It's outrageous that Caesar behaves so grandly," Cassius exclaimed. "He acts as if he's above us all but he's not a god. He's just a man like you and me."

Brutus nodded. "Caesar is my friend but success has made him too ambitious. For hundreds of years Rome has been a republic, governed by its free people. If we let one man become king to rule us again then Roman citizens will be no better than slaves."

Cassius looked over his shoulder to make sure nobody else could hear. "Then something must be done to stop Caesar," he said.

JULIUS
CAESAR

JULIUS
CAESAR

"Something must be done to protect our freedom," Brutus agreed with a troubled frown.

That night, there was a violent storm. People were afraid it was an omen of something bad to come. The city was deserted as Cassius's servant hurried through the dark, rainy streets carrying letters for Brutus. The letters appeared to be from worried citizens urging Brutus to save them from Caesar's rule but they were really written by Cassius, who hoped to turn Brutus against Caesar.

As Brutus brooded over the letters, meteors streaked across the sky, filling the night with such light that he could read without a candle. Brutus struggled to decide what to do. The only way to get rid of Caesar was to murder him but Brutus had no wish to kill his friend. Yet he was afraid that if Caesar was crowned King it would be a disaster for Rome. "Caesar is like a serpent's egg," he thought. "If left to hatch and grow he'll become a dangerous creature. Surely it's wise to save Rome by killing the serpent while it's in its shell?"

When the storm had passed, Brutus took a walk in his orchard. There he met Cassius, who'd come to see him with his fellow conspirators, Trebonius, Casca and others.

"Casca brings news that Caesar will be crowned King by the senators tomorrow," said Cassius. "It's time to act, Brutus. These men are prepared to kill Caesar. Are you with us?"

"Caesar to rule Rome as King!" Brutus exclaimed. He knew then that he had to do something. With a heavy heart he agreed to join the others. "Long ago, my ancestors drove the last treacherous king from this land," he said. "I promise Rome that I will protect it now."

The following day was the Ides of March. Caesar and Mark Antony, his closest friend and trusted general, travelled to the Temple where he was to be crowned. When they arrived, Trebonius drew Mark Antony away, while Cassius, Brutus and the others crowded around Caesar as if wishing to talk with him.

"Today our hands speak for us!" Casca cried and at these words the conspirators pulled out their daggers and stabbed Caesar many times. Last to strike was Brutus.

Caesar fell to the ground, his life ebbing away. He stared up at his friend. "Even you, Brutus?" he gasped weakly and with that he died.

At once a shout went up. "Caesar is dead!"

The other senators drew back in horror. "Don't be afraid," said Brutus. "Caesar's death was a sacrifice to save Rome. We acted out of love for our republic."

At that moment Mark Antony appeared. He stared in horror at Caesar, lying at the foot of the temple steps, and then at the bloodstained senators. "If you wish to kill me too then do it," he cried, baring his chest. "There is no better place to die than here at Caesar's side!"

Brutus assured Mark Antony that they wished him no harm. "You see blood on our hands but you cannot see the pity in our hearts," he told him. "When we explain ourselves to the people you'll understand the reason for what we've done."

Mark Antony looked each one of them in the eye. "If you can satisfy me that you had good cause for this then I shall be your friend," he told them. "I only ask to take Caesar's body and speak at his funeral."

Cassius was suspicious. "Don't let Mark Antony speak to the people, he may stir them up against us," he told Brutus.

JULIUS
CAESAR

But Brutus was trusting. "Have no fear," he replied. "I'll speak first and explain everything." Then Brutus and his followers left Mark Antony to attend to Caesar's body.

Mark Antony knelt in respect beside his lifeless friend. "Here are the ruins of the noblest man that ever lived," he cried. "I swear that anger and war will follow this foul deed."

Caesar's body was covered with a shroud and taken to the market square, where a great crowd had gathered, demanding to know what had happened.

Brutus spoke first. "Fellow Romans, you know that I am an honourable man," he began. "I didn't commit this terrible act because I loved Caesar any less than you do, but because I love Rome more. Caesar had grown ruthless and ambitious. His rule threatened to end our right to govern ourselves, so we did what was necessary to protect our freedom. If anyone feels that I've been unjust then I'll use the same dagger to end my own life."

The crowd muttered amongst themselves. They trusted Brutus and believed that he'd acted in the best interest of Rome. "Brutus must live!" they cried and they called for statues to be made in his honour. Relieved to have the support of the people, Brutus left them and went home.

Then it was Mark Antony's turn to speak.

Mark Antony stood sorrowfully beside Caesar's shrouded body. "Friends, Romans and countrymen," he said, "I am not here to speak fine words like honourable Brutus, but to mourn my friend and tell you how much Caesar loved you." He waved a scroll before the crowd. "Here, the proof is written in his will."

"Read it!" the crowd demanded.

But Mark Antony shook his head. "First let Caesar's wounds speak," he said and he pulled back the shroud. The crowd gasped in horror at the sight of Caesar's body. "Here is where honourable Brutus showed his love for Caesar," said Mark Antony. "And this is the mark of his good friend Cassius."

"How could Brutus be so cruel?" the people cried.

"In his will, Caesar left money to each one of you," continued Mark Antony. "He instructed that his parks and gardens should be made public for you all to enjoy. Is this the wish of a man who wanted to take away your freedom?"

"We've been tricked by Brutus and his friends!" cried a voice in the crowd. "They aren't honourable men, they're traitors."

JULIUS
CAESAR

"Give us Caesar's body," shouted another, "we'll use his funeral fire to burn down their houses." With angry protest the crowd hurried off to search for the conspirators.

"Now let revenge do its work," said Mark Antony.

Brutus and Cassius heard the uproar in the streets with alarm. They guessed that Mark Antony had turned the people against them. Moving fast, they fled the city.

Caesar's death stirred up chaos. People rioted for days, houses were burned and citizens fought against each other. Nobody could restore order in Rome until Caesar's young heir, his nephew Octavius, arrived with an army. Octavius went at once to see Mark Antony and together they took control of the city.

Brutus and Cassius knew that it wouldn't be long before they were pursued. They gathered their own armies and waited for the mighty forces of Rome. Soon, they heard news that Octavius and Mark Antony were approaching.

"Should we march out in the morning to meet them?" suggested Brutus.

"No," said Cassius. "Let our men rest and our enemies weary themselves by marching further."

But Brutus sensed that the day of battle had come. "Our legions are brim-full and our cause is ripe. If we don't act on this tide of fortune we may be lost with the current against us," he said.

So Cassius agreed.

On the morning of battle, Cassius saw birds of prey circling above their camp. "This is a bad omen," he thought but he kept his fears to himself.

Brutus agreed to face Octavius and Cassius prepared to fight Mark Antony. They wished each other good luck. "Today we must finish what the Ides of March began," said Brutus. "We may never meet again, old friend, so let us say goodbye."

That day, Brutus and his army won a victory against Octavius, but Cassius's men were defeated. His soldiers ran from the battlefield and the news came that Mark Antony had entered his camp.

Cassius sent his friend, Titinius, to the camp to confirm whether the news was true but a

JULIUS
CAESAR

short while later a messenger came to report that Titinius himself had been captured. Cassius remembered the fateful birds that he'd seen that morning. "All is lost," he declared. Rather than return to Rome in prisoner's chains, he took his own sword and killed himself.

However, the messenger had been mistaken; it was not Mark Antony who had entered the camp but Brutus and his men. Moments later Titinius returned bearing a victory wreath from Brutus, but it was too late for Cassius. So Titinius laid the wreath upon Cassius's head.

When Brutus arrived and saw what had happened he wept. "Rome will never produce such fine men again," he said and he ordered the body of Cassius to be taken away, so that the soldiers wouldn't be disheartened and give up the fight.

Then Brutus gathered his men for a second battle that day against Mark Antony's army. The rebels fought valiantly but the battle was lost. Exhausted and without hope, Brutus thanked his loyal men. "There is more glory in losing this noble fight than Octavius and Mark Antony gain by winning," he told them. "We have fought hard for our beloved Rome." Then he told them to flee for their lives.

One man alone chose to stay with him.

"My bones are ready to rest," sighed Brutus. "Hold my sword, farewell friend." And he plunged the blade into his heart.

When Octavius and Mark Antony found Brutus's body they felt no triumph.

"This was the noblest Roman of them all," said Mark Antony sadly. "Those other conspirators murdered Caesar out of jealousy but Brutus only acted in the interests of the people and the republic that he loved. Nature made him the finest man."

"Then he shall rest like a soldier in my own tent," said Octavius, "and we will bury him with all the respect an honourable Roman deserves."

JULIUS CAESAR

"Thou and I are too wise to woo peaceably."

MUCH
ADO
ABOUT NOTHING

CAST OF CHARACTERS

Hero
The Duke of Messina's
daughter

Don Pedro
A nobleman from
Aragon

Don John
Don Pedro's
brother

Beatrice
Hero's cousin

Benedick
A soldier and
nobleman

Claudio
A soldier who fought
under Don Pedro

MUCH ADO
ABOUT NOTHING

MUCH ADO ABOUT NOTHING

It was a day of excitement at the beautiful country estate of Leonato, the Governor of Messina. Leonato's old friend, Don Pedro, and his men were coming to visit on their journey home from war.

"It seems an age since they stayed with us on their way to fight," Leonato said to his daughter, Hero. "I hear that Claudio, the young man who showed you so much attention, has won great honour as a soldier."

Hero's heart quickened when she heard Claudio's name.

"Will Signor Benedick be with them?" asked Leonato's niece, Beatrice.

Leonato nodded with a smile. Whenever Beatrice and Benedick met there was a merry war between them as they tried to outdo each other with their sharp tongues and clever wit.

"I wonder who Benedick's favourite companion will be this month," said Beatrice. "He changes friends as often as he changes hats."

Hero laughed at her lively cousin. "I see he's not in your good books," she said.

"If Benedick was in my good books then I'd burn down my library!" Beatrice replied with a grin.

When Don Pedro and his men arrived that afternoon there was a high-spirited, happy reunion of friends. Beautiful Hero caught Claudio's eye and they gazed at each other admiringly.

Benedick greeted Beatrice with a bow. "Why, my dear Lady Scorn, are you still here?" he asked.

"How could I miss your visit, my lord, when you give me so much to be scornful of?" she said with a sweet smile.

Benedick sighed. "All the ladies love me except you," he said, "although I must be hard

MUCH ADO ABOUT NOTHING

97

hearted, for I don't love any of them."

"Well, that's good news for women," snapped Beatrice. "It spares them the trouble of a husband like you. I would rather hear my dog bark at a crow than hear a man telling me that he loves me."

"Excellent!" declared Benedick. "You are saving some poor gentleman from the scratch of your claws!"

Leonato and Don Pedro laughed at their jest.

"You must all stay with us for a month," insisted Leonato. "We shall have a masked ball this evening in your honour."

Don Pedro warmly accepted his old friend's invitation and so did everyone in his company. But one man stood apart, sullen-faced; Don Pedro's brother, Don John, thanked his host with cold politeness. He was a man who had no desire for pleasure.

That evening, Don John didn't join the others for dinner. His companion, Borachio, came to his room later with some gossip.

"Claudio wishes to marry Hero," he told Don John. "I overheard him asking for your brother's help."

MUCH ADO ABOUT NOTHING

Don John listened with interest. He hated being dependent upon his wealthy brother and was looking for an opportunity for revenge against Claudio, who had become Don Pedro's new favourite. "There may be a chance for mischief here," he said thoughtfully.

At the masked ball that evening, there was plenty of opportunity for mischief.

The guests teased each other with their disguises. Beatrice pretended not to recognise Benedick. "Do you know Signor Benedick?" she asked as they danced together. "He's Don Pedro's jester, a very dull fool."

Benedick swung her firmly around. "No," he said, frowning behind his mask. "But if we

meet, I'll tell him how little you think of him."

When she'd left him, Benedick complained to Don Pedro. "The Lady Beatrice has called me a dull fool," he said. "She hurled so many insults at me that I felt like a shooting target." Don Pedro wasn't fooled by the sharp words that flew between Beatrice and Benedick. He was sure that they liked each other, even though they hid it well. However, when he tried to make peace between them during the evening they both outwitted him.

"I'd rather be sent on an errand to the end of the world than befriend my lady Beatrice," said Benedick. "Send me to fetch you a toothpick from the furthest inch of Asia."

"I was born to speak all mirth and no matter," Beatrice insisted with a merry smile.

Don Pedro had more success in his matchmaking with Claudio and Hero. By the end of the night, Claudio had confessed his love to Hero and won her heart. With joy, she agreed to marry him and her father was delighted to give the couple his blessing. Claudio was eager to wed Hero the very next day but Leonato insisted that they wait a week while arrangements were made.

"Don't look disappointed," Don Pedro told Claudio. "I have an idea for passing the time until the wedding. Let's work together to persuade Beatrice and Benedick to fall in love with each other. They both swear they are against marriage but anyone can see they are a perfect match."

"I'll do anything to find a good husband for my cousin," said Hero and Leonato and Claudio agreed to help.

"Then I shall tell you my plan," said Don Pedro. "If we succeed in this, Cupid can hang up his bow, for we shall be the gods of love!"

Don John received the news of Claudio's engagement with a villainous scowl. "What can we do to upset this wedding?" he asked Borachio.

Borachio had a suggestion. At their last visit to Leonato's house he had befriended Hero's maid. "The night before the wedding, I'll ask her to come to her mistress's bedroom window," he said. "Then I'll climb up from the garden and sweet talk her, so it appears as if I am wooing

MUCH ADO ABOUT NOTHING

Hero herself. Meanwhile, you tell Don Pedro and Claudio that Hero is being unfaithful and bring them to see the evidence before their eyes. Jealousy should do the rest."

Don John liked what he heard.

Meanwhile, the following day, Don Pedro lost no time in putting his own plan into action.

Benedick took a walk in the garden, bemoaning the change in his friend, Claudio. "All day he mopes about listening to minstrels playing love songs and talking about romance," Benedick grumbled to himself. "Huh! I'll never let love change me!"

He didn't notice Don Pedro, Leonato and Claudio hide themselves behind a high hedge nearby. As Benedick came close they began to talk loudly, so as to be overheard.

"Tell me, Leonato," said Don Pedro, "is it true that your niece Beatrice is in love with Signor Benedick?"

Benedick stopped in surprise. He crept close to listen.

"I never thought she would love any man," said Claudio.

"Me neither," said Leonato, "but it seems that she loves him with a passion. Unfortunately it's a tragic case. Beatrice says that she'll die if Benedick doesn't love her and yet she'd rather die than tell him how she feels. The poor girl is afraid that Benedick will only mock her feelings."

"Should we tell him?" asked Claudio.

"No, no," said Don Pedro. "Hopefully her love will cool with time. Benedick is my good friend, but he's not worthy of such an excellent lady as Beatrice."

With Cupid's work done, the three friends walked back to the house.

Benedick was struck with wonder. "Beatrice loves me!" he exclaimed. "Well then, her love must be requited. It's true that she is a most excellent lady. People may laugh at me for loving her as I've spoken against marriage for so long, but any man can change his mind."

Suddenly, to his delight, Beatrice appeared. Benedick greeted her with a smile. "She is much more beautiful than her cousin, Hero," he thought to himself.

Beatrice strode up to him with her hands on her hips. "Against my will I have been sent to tell you that lunch is ready," she said.

"I thank you for your pains," said Benedick, still smiling.

"If it had been painful, I would not have come," said Beatrice.

"So you took pleasure in the message?" said Benedick.

"About as much pleasure as one might take in choking a bird," said Beatrice, thinking that Benedick was acting very strangely today. Then, without waiting for a reply, she flounced off.

"Hmm…" Benedick pondered on her words. "'Against my will I have been sent to tell you that lunch is ready.' I'm sure there must be a double meaning in that. If I don't love her, I'm a fool!"

Later that day, Hero sent a message asking Beatrice to join her in the garden. When Beatrice went outside she heard her name being whispered. Hero was talking to her ladies-maid in a hushed tone. Beatrice hid behind a statue to listen.

"Are you sure that Signor Benedick loves Lady Beatrice?" the maid asked her mistress.

"Yes, Claudio told me," said Hero sounding surprised. "But I've told him that Benedick must look for a wife elsewhere, for Beatrice is far too proud to love anyone."

"It's true," the maid agreed. "They say Signor Benedick is the most desirable bachelor in Italy but I'm sure Lady Beatrice would only make a mockery of his love."

MUCH ADO
ABOUT NOTHING

Hero sighed loudly. "It's such a shame. Benedick is an excellent man," she said. And with that the two women walked away, leaving Beatrice dumbstruck.

"Benedick loves me!" she thought and her heart leapt. "How can people think I'm too proud to feel the same? Well, they'll soon see how easily I can requite his love. It's true, he is an excellent man!"

Next day, Don Pedro and Claudio were laughing at how Benedick had suddenly taken to sighing like a love-struck schoolboy, when Don John came to speak to them.

"I have troubling news of the lady Hero," Don John said darkly. "She is disloyal to you, Claudio."

"Disloyal?" Claudio couldn't believe it.

"I have proof that Hero loves another man," said Don John. "Meet me in the garden at midnight. When you see the evidence you may wish to save yourself from an unwise marriage tomorrow."

Full of dismay, Claudio and Don Pedro agreed. When they met Don John that night, they looked up at Hero's window, and were shocked to see Borachio whispering words of love to a shadowy figure they mistook for Hero herself. However, the woman they saw was really Hero's maid who had no idea she was being used to deceive Claudio. As Borachio intended, Claudio

was broken-hearted. He vowed to Don Pedro that he would meet Hero at the chapel next day as planned and then confront her with the shameful truth of her betrayal.

Next morning the wedding guests gathered in Leonato's chapel. Claudio waited, stony-faced, for his bride. When Hero arrived, the Friar asked if anyone had an objection to the marriage.

Claudio turned to him. "Hero has given her heart to another man," he declared.

Hero stared in bewilderment.

"It is true," said Don Pedro. "We both saw Hero talk of love to another man from her window last night."

"But I didn't talk to anyone," cried Hero.

"Liar!" shouted Don John.

Hero saw the look of deep disappointment on Claudio's face and fainted into her father's arms. As Beatrice and the Friar rushed to her side, Claudio and his friends marched out of the chapel.

MUCH ADO
ABOUT NOTHING

Only Benedick stayed behind. "Is Hero dead?" he asked.

"No," said the Friar but it gave him an idea. "Maybe it would help if we pretend that Hero is dead for a while," he suggested. "I'm sure in grief, Claudio would regret his accusations and remember his love. It would give us time to find out where this false rumour began."

Everyone agreed to the Friar's plan. As Leonato took Hero home, Benedick waited behind to tell Beatrice of his love.

"Here's a strange thing my Lady," he said. "Against my will, I find that I love nothing in the world so much as you."

Beatrice pretended to be surprised. "Well, it's as strange as this," she replied, "that I love you, Sir, with so much of my heart there is none left to protest!"

Benedick took her hand in his. "Then I will live in your heart, Beatrice, and be buried in your eyes," he said happily.

Back at the house, the local constable arrived with news that Borachio had been arrested after drunkenly bragging about his deception. "So, Claudio was tricked," said Leonato thoughtfully.

When Claudio heard that Hero was dead and that he had been deceived by Don John he was full of deep remorse. "My mistrust killed Hero," he told Leonato miserably. "You must choose what punishment you like."

Leonato listened with a grave expression. "My brother has an unmarried daughter who looks very like Hero," he told Claudio. "If you marry this lady, then I will forgive you." Claudio agreed.

The next day, Claudio and Don Pedro returned to the chapel in a sombre mood. Leonato brought in the bride, wearing a veil over her face.

"Will you take this woman to be your wife?" asked the Friar.

"Yes," said Claudio, as he'd promised.

His new wife lifted her veil and Hero gazed back at him.

Claudio gasped in amazement. "My Hero, come back from the dead!"

"She was only dead while suspicion lived," said Leonato and he embraced them both.

Benedick stepped forward. "Will you marry me, Beatrice?" he asked.

"Only to save your life," she replied, "as I'm told you will die otherwise."

"So, I shall marry you," he said, "but only out of pity, you understand," and he gave her a kiss.

Then everyone laughed to see that Beatrice and Benedick had not lost their wit in love.

All that day, wedding celebrations filled the air with music and laughter. As the guests danced among the meadows and vineyards, Don John slipped away. The party continued on late into the night, for no one knew how to make merry better than the friends and family of Leonato.

MUCH ADO
ABOUT NOTHING

"As flies to wanton boys are we to th' gods:
They kill us for their sport."

KING LEAR

CAST OF CHARACTERS

King Lear
Ruler of Britain

Gonerill
King Lear's eldest
daughter

Regan
King Lear's middle
daughter

Cordelia
King Lear's youngest
daughter

Earl of Gloucester
A nobleman loyal to
King Lear

Edgar
The Earl of Gloucester's
first-born son and heir

KING LEAR

King Lear had grown old and frail. He sent for his three daughters.

"I have ruled Britain for many years," he told them, "now I wish for a life without royal duties. I've decided to divide my kingdom between you. The largest share will be given to the daughter who loves me most."

Lear's eldest daughter, Gonerill, was eager to have the largest share of the kingdom. "I love you more than sight, sound and even breath," she told the King.

Her sister, Regan, also wanted the largest part. "I love you as much as Gonerill does and more!" she insisted. "The only thing that makes me happy is your love."

The King nodded with satisfaction. Then he turned to his youngest daughter, Cordelia, who was his favourite. Cordelia was the kindest of his three daughters and the King hoped that she would look after him in his old age. "What can you say to win more of my kingdom than Gonerill and Regan?" he asked her.

"Nothing," replied Cordelia.

The King was taken aback. "Nothing?" he cried. "Nothing will win you nothing!"

However, Cordelia was more honest than her sisters. "I love you as much as a daughter should love her father," she said truthfully. "Gonerill and Regan claim that all their love is for you, yet they are both married. When I marry, half my love will be for my husband."

At these words King Lear flew into a rage. "If that is the truth, then the truth is all you shall have, Cordelia!" he cried angrily. "As you refuse to please me you are no longer my daughter."

Despite the protests of his close advisors, Lear banished Cordelia from his sight forever, without a penny to her name.

Cordelia left, deeply sad and shocked at her father's cruel punishment.

KING LEAR

Then Lear divided his kingdom between Gonerill and Regan. "For myself, I shall only keep a hundred knights," he told them, "and I will live with each of you in turn, a month at a time."

King Lear's angry outburst was witnessed by his old friend, the Earl of Gloucester, who returned to his castle troubled by what he had seen. As Gloucester entered the great hall he saw his youngest son, Edmund, conceal a letter behind his back.

"What are you hiding from me?" he asked.

"Nothing, Father," said Edmund innocently. "It's just a letter from my brother, Edgar." But Edmund's reluctance to share the letter made Gloucester suspicious and he demanded to see it.

As Gloucester read, he stared in disbelief. "It says here that Edgar is impatient to inherit my fortune, so he plots to murder me and asks for your help! Can such treachery really be true?" he asked Edmund.

"I'm sure Edgar is only trying to test my loyalty, Father," Edmund replied. But Gloucester was so outraged that he went to order his men to arrest Edgar at once.

When he'd gone, Edmund smiled wickedly, for the letter was a fake that he'd written to trick his father. "Why should I be deprived of an inheritance just because I'm the youngest son?" he thought jealously. "I am as worthy as my brother." Driven by a ruthless ambition, Edmund intended to destroy Edgar and his father so that he could have the family fortune for himself.

When Edgar learned that his father had turned against him he fled from the castle. To avoid capture he exchanged his fine clothes for rags and roamed the wild countryside, disguised as a beggar called Tom.

KING LEAR

Meanwhile, King Lear and his men went to live with Gonerill. However, it wasn't long before she began to complain about the hundred knights she was expected to provide for.

"Your men are a disorderly rabble," she told him sternly. "They constantly quarrel and cause a riot. I've ordered half of them to be dismissed."

The King was cross at being overruled by his daughter and treated with no respect. "Your ungrateful heart is as cold as marble, Gonerill," he said bitterly. "At least I have one more daughter who will offer me comfort." So he left with his remaining knights to visit Regan.

However, Gonerill sent a messenger to warn Regan that the King and his men were coming. By the time they arrived at her palace, Regan was gone.

King Lear and his knights travelled instead to the Earl of Gloucester's castle where, to his surprise, he found Regan had been welcomed as a guest.

The King complained to her about Gonerill. "Your sister dismissed half my knights," he protested. "Her sharp-toothed unkindness sits on my heart like a vulture."

But Regan showed her father no sympathy. "I'm sure Gonerill had good reason," she said coldly. "You are an old man and need the wisdom of somebody who knows better. Return to Gonerill and ask for her forgiveness."

"Never!" cried the King. "I would rather live in the wilderness with a wolf!"

"Well, you can't bring fifty knights to stay with me," Regan told him. "I don't see why you need an army at all. Get rid of it, my own men will attend you."

The King exploded with frustration. "I gave you everything," he roared. "How can you deny me what I have left? You are as wicked as your sister. Your love is a lie." He called on the gods for revenge.

As if in answer, thunder shook the castle and lightning flashed across the sky. "I think I shall go mad!" cried Lear, enraged, and he ran out into the storm.

Gloucester started to go after his frail old friend but Regan stood in his way.

"Let him go," she insisted. "He has brought this on himself."

Gloucester was horrified at her cruelty but he had to obey.

All night, Lear stumbled through the cold wind and lashing rain. Tormented by the treachery of his eldest daughters and the loss of Cordelia, he began to lose his mind. In distress he tore at his hair, crying out to the storm to destroy the world.

"Rumble your bellyful!" he commanded the thunder. "Spout, rain! Spit, fire!" he roared at the sky.

At last, utterly exhausted, Lear came to a lonely barn. Inside, crouched among the hay, he found Edgar, disguised as a beggar, sheltering from the storm.

Lear was stirred by the sight of the beggar, alone in the world like himself. No longer filled with anger, he was overcome with pity. "I have taken too little care of the homeless and poor in my life," he thought sorrowfully. "What is your name?" he asked.

"Poor Tom's a-cold," Edgar whimpered. "Poor Tom's a-cold."

King Lear sat down in the hay beside Edgar, his body weak and his mind troubled. "I see now that man is really no more than a poor, bare, two-legged animal," he thought to himself. "This is what it truly means to have nothing."

KING LEAR

As dawn rose, the storm subsided. Out of the morning mist, Gloucester approached the barn. He had defied Regan and come looking for his old friend. Gloucester didn't recognise his son in beggars' rags but he was saddened to find the King, lying helpless and confused.

Gloucester's men carried Lear into a carriage. "I've received a letter from Cordelia," Gloucester told him. "She married the King of France and has arrived in Dover with a French army to win back the kingdom from her sisters." Then he told his men to take Lear in haste to Dover.

"The King will be safe now," Gloucester told Edgar, "but I am sad to see his madness. I tell you, friend, that I am almost mad with grief myself, for I have lost a son, who I loved with all my heart."

Edgar saw the deep sorrow in his father's eyes, but he was not ready to reveal his true identity. All he replied was "Poor Tom's a-cold."

Gloucester returned to his castle. To his surprise, he was met by Gonerill and Regan who had him arrested at once. Edmund had betrayed his father by showing them Cordelia's letter from Dover. The two sisters ordered Gloucester to be blinded as punishment for his treachery.

Sightless, Gloucester called out for help. "Where is my son, Edmund?"

Regan laughed cruelly. "Don't bother calling for him," she said. "Edmund hates you. He was the one who betrayed you!" Then blind Gloucester saw the truth; Edgar was innocent and he had allowed himself to be wickedly deceived.

Gloucester's old servant took pity on him and gently led him away. "I'll find someone to be your eyes, my lord," he said and he took him to Tom the beggar.

Edgar was horrified when his father appeared before him, blind and helpless. But Gloucester didn't want any pity.

"I no longer need sight," he sighed. "When I had my eyes I didn't see the truth. If only I could touch the son I treated so wrongly, then that would be far better to me than sight." He asked the beggar if he would lead him to Dover, to be with the King.

With a heavy heart, Edgar took his father's hand and they set off together.

Meanwhile, at Dover, Lear was reunited with Cordelia. Although suffering and loss had weakened his mind, it had also taught him wisdom. He fell to his knees before his daughter. "I am a foolish old man," he said humbly. "I know you have good reason not to love me, Cordelia, but can you forgive and forget?"

Cordelia wept to see her father so changed. She knelt beside him and kissed his hand. "I love you as a daughter should love her father," she assured him. "I will look after you." Cordelia found lodgings for him and prepared her army for battle against her sisters.

Gonerill and Regan joined their forces with Edmund's men for the fight. On the day of the battle, they had the greater strength and Cordelia's French army was defeated. Lear and Cordelia were captured.

"Don't weep," Lear told his daughter as they were led to prison. "We shall be happy together without any cares, singing like two birds in a cage."

But Edmund had a different fate in mind for them both. More ambitious than ever, he planned to seize power from Gonerill and Regan and didn't want any trouble from Lear and Cordelia. He sent a messenger to the gaoler, with instructions that both the prisoners should be murdered.

However, just as the messenger hurried away, Edgar appeared in full armour, his helmet hiding his face. He stepped forward to challenge Edmund.

"You have betrayed your brother and your father," Edgar cried. "You are a traitor, from the crown of your head to the dust beneath your feet!"

At once Edmund took up his sword and lunged at the stranger, but Edgar was more skilful

KING LEAR

KING LEAR

in combat. He delivered Edmund a fatal wound.

"If I must die by your sword, then at least tell me your name," gasped Edmund.

Edgar lifted his visor. "I am the son of Gloucester," he said, "the father who was blinded for your treachery and died today of a broken heart."

Edmund sighed deeply. "So, it has all come to nothing," he said, realising the tragic consequence of his jealous greed for power. "Hurry to the gaol brother. I sent an order that Lear and Cordelia should be killed today. Save them if you can! With my last breath I may do some good."

But Edmund's change of heart was too late. Although a messenger hurried to the prison he wasn't in time to save Cordelia. King Lear returned, ashen-faced, carrying her lifeless body.

"A plague upon you, murderers and traitors!" he said, weeping. "My poor Cordelia will never live again." For a moment the old King bent close as if he heard her softly speak, then overcome with grief, he collapsed to the ground and died, with his beloved, faithful daughter in his arms.

KING LEAR

"…let the forfeit
Be nominated for an equal pound
Of your fair flesh, to be cut off and taken
In what part of your body pleaseth me."

CAST OF CHARACTERS

Bassanio
A young gentleman and
friend of Antonio

Antonio
A merchant of
Venice

Portia
A wealthy noblewoman
from Belmont

Shylock
A moneylender of
Venice

Nerissa
Portia's maid

Gratiano
Bassanio's friend

THE MERCHANT
OF VENICE

THE MERCHANT OF VENICE

Sunlight sparkled on the canals of Venice as a young gentleman called Bassanio walked with his friend, the merchant Antonio.

Bassanio had a secret to share. "I've fallen in love, with a wonderful lady called Portia," he told Antonio. "She's clever and beautiful and I'm sure she likes me."

"Then why do you look so troubled?" asked Antonio.

Bassanio sighed. "Portia's father recently died and left her a fortune," he said. "Now Princes travel from far and wide to her palace in Belmont, hoping to marry her."

"Well, my friend, you know I'll do anything to help you," said Antonio.

"Money is what I need," explained Bassanio. "If I could buy fine clothes and gifts for Portia, then maybe I'd have a chance against my rivals."

Antonio nodded thoughtfully. "I have no money until my ships sell their goods and return to Venice," he said. "But people know I'm trustworthy. Find someone who will lend

THE MERCHANT OF VENICE

117

you the money you need and I'll promise to pay it back when my ships come home."

Bassanio's face lit up. He thanked Antonio. "When I'm married to Portia all my debts will be paid!" he said happily and with hope in his heart he went off to find someone who would give him a loan.

At the market place he met Shylock, the moneylender. Shylock was reluctant to help Bassanio at first, but when he heard that the money would be repaid by Antonio, he became very interested.

"This may be a way to get my revenge on Antonio," Shylock thought to himself. "How I loathe him. He steals my business by lending money without a charge and speaks ill of me to the other merchants." But Shylock showed none of his hatred to Bassanio.

"Let us discuss what you need," he said.

At that moment, Antonio himself appeared. He was dismayed to find Bassanio talking business with the moneylender whose greed he despised.

"Well, Shylock," said Antonio briskly, "will you lend three thousand ducats to my friend here?"

Shylock stroked his long beard. "Signor Antonio," he said, "many times you have called me a cut-throat dog."

"No doubt I'll call you the same again," said Antonio. "But this is business. If I fail to repay the loan think how much you'll enjoy demanding a penalty from your enemy."

"I only wish to have your love and goodwill," said Shylock slyly. "To show my friendship I

THE MERCHANT
OF VENICE

will lend you the money without charge."

Bassanio sighed with relief.

"But if the loan is not paid back exactly three months from now," continued Shylock, "you must pay a penalty – a pound of your flesh, Antonio, cut from a place nearest your heart."

Bassanio's relief turned to horror. "I won't let you agree to that, Antonio!" he cried.

Shylock looked offended. "But I make this offer in friendship, gentlemen," he said. "If my money is not repaid all I gain is a pound of flesh which is worth nothing at all."

Although Antonio knew that Shylock's friendship was false, he could not refuse the money-lender's challenge. Determined to help Bassanio, he agreed to accept the conditions of the loan. "My ships will return long before the money is due to be repaid," he assured his friend.

Bassanio took Shylock's money and bought fine clothes for himself and gifts for Portia. His friend Gratiano, who had accompanied him on his first trip to Belmont, was also eager to return, so they set sail together.

While Bassanio and Gratiano travelled towards Belmont, Portia was growing tired of all the unsuitable men who came to visit, hoping to marry her. Before her father died, he'd given her three caskets – one made of gold, one of silver and one of lead – and insisted that only the man who could guess which casket contained Portia's portrait should marry his daughter.

"It's so hard not to be able to choose a husband for myself," Portia said as her maid, Nerissa, set out the caskets for the arrival of the Prince of Morocco.

"If I was to choose a husband for you, my lady, it would be that handsome man who came from Venice to visit your father," replied Nerissa mischievously.

Portia remembered the young Venetian very well. "Yes, Bassanio was his name, wasn't it?" she said. "He was certainly handsome." And she turned from Nerissa to hide her blushes.

When the Prince of Morocco entered, Portia told him of her father's test. "One of these three caskets contains my portrait, Prince. If you choose that one then I will be your wife."

The Prince of Morocco accepted the challenge. First, he read the inscription on the casket of lead. "Whoever chooses me must risk all he has."

"No man of wealth would risk all he has for worthless lead!" scoffed the Prince, so he turned to the silver casket.

"Whoever chooses me will get what he deserves," he read. "I'm a man of noble birth and deserve the finest things, so surely I deserve the Lady Portia," he thought to himself. But to be sure, he read the inscription on the gold casket.

"Whoever chooses me will get what many men desire." The Prince smiled. "Many men come to gaze at your beauty, my Lady," he said to Portia. "This must be the right choice."

However, to the Prince's dismay, the casket only contained a skull with a note beside it.

"All that glistens is not gold," he read. The Prince of Morocco realised that he'd been unwise to choose by appearances. With a heavy heart he departed.

A short while later, the Prince of Aragon arrived. He studied the caskets carefully. Like the Prince of Morocco, he refused to risk anything for a casket of lead. He also dismissed the casket of gold.

"I won't choose what many men desire," he said, "because most men are fools." So he turned to the silver casket. "Whoever chooses me shall get what he deserves. Well, that's just how it should be," he decided. "And I deserve the best!" The Prince opened it up but he was disappointed to find the portrait of a jester inside.

THE MERCHANT OF VENICE

"It seems I came here with one fool's head and I go away with two," he said sadly.

Portia heaved a sigh of relief as she watched him go. However, Nerissa hardly had time to put the caskets away when a messenger announced that another suitor had arrived from Venice. "Please let it be Lord Bassanio," she whispered to herself.

Portia and Bassanio greeted each other with great joy. As Nerissa had suspected, Bassanio had won her mistress's heart the moment they first met and now he confessed that he'd thought of nothing but Portia since that day. Bassanio told Portia how his good friend Antonio had helped him but she only cared that he loved her as much as she loved him. However, they could not be married unless Bassanio faced her father's test and chose correctly.

Nerissa set the three caskets before him.

"I am locked in one of them," said Portia. "If you love me, you will find me." Portia desperately wished that she could tell Bassanio which casket to choose but all she could do was watch silently and trust that her father's test would bring her true love's happiness.

Bassanio studied the caskets thoughtfully. He wasn't tempted by the shining gold and silver. "Beauty can't be trusted," he said, "it's often used to disguise something ugly. But the lead casket promises nothing; it only asks that I risk all that I have, which I willingly do for love." To Portia's delight, he opened the lead casket and found her portrait inside.

"Myself, and all that is mine, I give to you," said Portia. Nerissa and Gratiano smiled at each other and congratulated them.

"Well, now at last I can marry too," announced Gratiano and he revealed that he and Nerissa had also fallen in love the day they first met. "Nerissa vowed not to marry me unless Bassanio wed her mistress," he explained. "So I thank your lordship for giving me a wife!"

Their two weddings soon followed. But a month later, a letter arrived that cut short everyone's happiness.

"Antonio's ships have all been wrecked," Bassanio read aghast. "Our loan hasn't been repaid on time, so now Shylock is demanding his pound of flesh!"

"You must hurry to help your friend," said Portia. "We have gold to pay the debt twenty times over."

Bassanio and Gratiano set sail at once for Venice.

Unable to pay his debt, Antonio had been arrested and locked up. From his prison cell, he tried to reason with Shylock, but the cruel moneylender showed him no pity.

"The law must give me justice," Shylock said. "I'll have my pound of flesh. You called me a dog, Antonio, well now you'll see my fangs!"

Meanwhile, Portia came up with her own plan to help Antonio. "After all, we owe him our happiness," she told Nerissa. First she took advice from her cousin, Doctor Bellario, who was a learned lawyer, and then she and Nerissa set off for Venice themselves.

On the day of Antonio's trial, he was brought to the courtroom, before the Duke of Venice.

"I'm sorry for you, Antonio," said the Duke. "Shylock is an inhuman wretch." But Antonio was resigned to his fate. He knew that his bargain must be kept. The law couldn't save him from Shylock's revenge.

When Shylock entered the courtroom, the Duke asked him to show mercy towards Antonio.

The moneylender cruelly refused. "I hate Antonio!" he said. "I only demand what is due to me."

THE MERCHANT OF VENICE

Then Bassanio stepped forward. "For your three thousand ducats I offer you six thousand," he said.

But Shylock just shrugged. "If you offered me six thousand times six thousand ducats I wouldn't take them," he said with a sneer. "I want my pound of flesh. Shall I have justice?"

The Duke told the court that he wished to wait until the learned lawyer, Doctor Bellario, arrived, before making a judgement. At that moment a young lawyer and his assistant arrived in court with a letter from Doctor Bellario. Bassanio and Gratiano didn't recognise their wives in disguise.

The Duke read the letter. "Doctor Bellario is unwell," he told the court, "so instead he has sent a brilliant young lawyer called Balthasar." The Duke asked Balthasar to speak.

Portia pressed her false beard firmly to her chin and stepped forward.

"I have read the details of this case," she said gruffly. "Antonio, do you agree that you owe money to this man, Shylock?" she asked. Antonio agreed. "Then the moneylender must be merciful," she said.

Shylock scowled. "Why should I?" he replied.

"Mercy is twice blessed," Portia told him. "It blesses the one who gives it and the one who

THE MERCHANT
OF VENICE

121

receives it."

"I don't care about mercy, I've done nothing wrong." Shylock shook his fists in frustration. "I only want the law!" he demanded.

Bassanio explained that he'd offered to repay the loan but his money had been refused. "Then the law says that Shylock has the right to his pound of flesh," announced Portia, "to be cut off near the merchant's heart."

Everyone in the court gasped. Shylock's eyes glinted with malice. He took a knife from his bag and began to sharpen it. The sight sent a chill through the crowd.

"Prepare yourself, Antonio," said Portia.

Shylock took a pair of scales out of his bag, ready to weigh the flesh, and grinned with wicked anticipation.

But as he raised his knife, Portia had a warning for him. "Take care, Shylock," she said. "The penalty you agreed to was a pound of flesh, but it said nothing of Antonio's blood. If you shed one single drop, the Duke has the right to take your life."

Shylock froze with the knife in his hand. He couldn't take what was owed to him without losing his own life! He realised that he'd been outwitted. "Then give me the money!" he cried.

"You've already refused it," said Portia firmly. "The law only grants you the penalty."

The moneylender cursed under his breath. Prevented from having his money or his revenge upon Antonio, Shylock slunk away, empty handed and humiliated.

Then Antonio was released. Although he wished to thank the young lawyer who had saved him, Portia and Nerissa hurried away from the court, to get home before their husbands.

When the two couples were reunited and the deception was revealed, there was much laughter in Belmont. Portia and Bassanio agreed that their happiness was now complete, with the freedom of their good friend Antonio, the merchant of Venice.

THE MERCHANT OF VENICE

ABOUT WILLIAM SHAKESPEARE

William Shakespeare was born in the English town of Stratford-upon-Avon, in 1564. When he was seven, he went to the local grammar school to study Maths, English, French and Latin, and was introduced to stories including the fables of Aesop, Greek myths and Ovid. His first experience of theatre was perhaps acting out Greek plays at school, or helping out with the visiting 'Mystery' and 'Miracle' plays of the time – religious pantomimes acted out by groups of craftsmen. William's father was a glove-maker, and at around age 15, he began to learn this craft. Not much of him is known after that until 1585 when William and his family moved to London, so that he could become an actor and a playwright!

By 1594, William had become a member of the best troupe of players in London: the Lord Chamberlain's Men. In his early days as an apprentice, he probably played small roles, swept up after the crowds had gone home and helped the actors dress. Another of his tasks may have been helping more experienced playwrights add new scenes to plays, and even coming up with his own ideas. One of his earliest performed works in 1590 was *The Taming of the Shrew*. This was followed by *The Comedy of Errors* and *The Gentleman of Verona*. Two of his best-loved plays, *Romeo and Juliet* and *A Midsummer Night's Dream*, were written soon after. Some of his plays were performed at court as well as for the public.

In 1599, the Lord Chamberlain's Men moved to a new theatre: The Globe. Here, many of Shakespeare's most famous plays were performed, including *Henry V*, *Hamlet*, *Othello* and *Twelfth Night*. His plays were popular for making audiences laugh one minute and weep the next and made Shakespeare a famous and wealthy man. He owned the second-biggest house in Stratford and other houses in London. In 1603 Queen Elizabeth died and King James I took the throne. Shakespeare's company was awarded a royal patent and became the King's Men. Shakespeare continued to write plays for The Globe, but also used an indoor theatre called Blackfriars in bad weather. His last great work, *The Tempest*, was performed there in 1613.

William Shakespeare died on 23rd April 1616. His plays are considered to be among the greatest works of literature ever written in the world, and are still performed regularly today.

FULL LIST OF PLAYS

COMEDIES

All's Well that Ends Well (1604-5)
As You Like It (1599-1600)
The Comedy of Errors (1594)
Love's Labour's Lost (1594-5)
Measure for Measure (1603-4)
The Merchant of Venice (1596-7)
The Merry Wives of Windsor (1597-8)
A Midsummer Night's Dream (1595)
Much Ado About Nothing (1598)
Pericles, Prince of Tyre (1607-8)
The Taming of the Shrew (1590-1)
The Tempest (1611)
Twelfth Night (1600-1)
The Two Gentleman of Verona (1590-1)
The Two Noble Kinsmen (1613-4)
The Winter's Tale (1609)

HISTORIES

Henry IV, Part 1 (1596-7)
Henry IV, Part 2 (1597-8)
Henry V (1598-9)
Henry VI, Part 1 (1591)
Henry VI, Part 2 (1591)
Henry VI, Part 3 (1591)
Henry VIII (1613)
King John (c.1595)
Richard II (1595)
Richard III (1593)

TRAGEDIES

Antony and Cleopatra (1606)
Coriolanus (1605–1608)
Cymbeline (1611)
Hamlet (1600-1)
Julius Caesar (1599)
King Lear (1605-6)
Macbeth (1606)
Othello (1603-4)
Romeo and Juliet (1595)
Timon of Athens (c.1608)
Titus Andronicus (1588-93)
Troilus and Cressida (1601)

ABOUT THE PLAYS IN THIS BOOK

As You Like It

During the 1590s Shakespeare wrote a number of comedies (plays that ended happily and made people laugh). In this one, Shakespeare makes fun of the ideas about love at the time, for example that love is a disease that brings suffering and torment. He also contrasts city life and country life, showing the forest to be a place where characters may be healed, away from the stresses of courtly life. It may be that the Forest of Arden was inspired by the real Forest of Arden, near where Shakespeare grew up!

Hamlet

At the beginning of this play, Hamlet sees his father's ghost who tells him that he was murdered, and asks him to avenge his death. Revenge plays were common at the time, but Shakespeare's *Hamlet* was different. Instead of there being lots of violent action, Hamlet's is unsure what to do. He questions whether he can trust the ghost, or has the courage to commit murder, and even starts to question the nature of life and death itself. It is this focus on Hamlet's thoughts that has made the play so famous.

Julius Caesar

For this play, Shakespeare focuses on real-life events: the assassination of Julius Caesar on March 15, 44 BCE. Here, he explores ideas of who should rule and how. Rome is a Republic ruled by a group of men called Senators who vote on its laws, but Caesar is becoming more and more like a king. The play is also about free will versus fate, as Caesar (like Macbeth) receives a prophecy at the beginning that foretells what will happen to him.

King Lear

King Lear is perhaps Shakespeare's darkest play of all. An elderly king allows his vanity to get the better of him, and leaves his kingdom to his two selfish daughters, rather than the one who loves him the most – Cordelia. When his daughters betray him, Lear slowly goes mad. Audiences find very little justice in this play, as at the end Lear is reunited with Cordelia, only for them to be defeated in battle and eventually die. There is goodness in the play, but it's hard to tell if it triumphs over evil or not.

Macbeth

Macbeth is a tale of how hunger for power can have tragic consequences. The prophecy of three witches begins a chain of events that leads to death and destruction, but it's never clear whether Macbeth is truly fated to be king, or just wills it to be so. *Macbeth* was one of the first plays performed for James I after the gunpowder plot of 1605 which tried to blow up the king's court. Some historians think it is a cautionary tale, warning any more would-be assassins of the consequences for their actions.

The Merchant of Venice

Justice and the law are two of the themes of this play. Mercy is another: Shylock's determination to have his 'pound of flesh' from Antonio, despite others asking him to be merciful, makes the audience think he is a villain. But is he also a victim of prejudice? Some people believe that *The Merchant of Venice* is

anti-semitic, in its portrayal of Shylock, who is Jewish. However, in one famous speech Shylock tells the audience that Jews are the same as anyone else: "If you prick us, do we not bleed? If you tickle us, do we not laugh? If you poison us, do we not die? And if you wrong us, shall we not revenge?"

A Midsummer Night's Dream
Written to celebrate a wealthy London wedding, *A Midsummer Night's Dream* is a comedy about mistaken identity and the difficulty of love. Four lovers are mixed up in a quarrel between the fairy king and queen with hilarious results. As Lysander points out, "The course of true love never did run smooth", but all is made well by Puck and a little magic. Light-hearted and fun, *A Midsummer Night's Dream* is one of Shakespeare's most popular plays today.

Much Ado About Nothing
Full of wit and good humour, this lively comedy tells the story of two couples: Benedick and Beatrice, and Hero and Claudio. It contains similar themes to Shakespeare's other comedies, such as mistaken identity and the obstacles to true love. What is unique about *Much Ado* is the witty conversation and polished social graces which characterised courtly life at the time. The relationship between Benedick and Beatrice is particularly spiky!

Othello
Jealousy and obsession are the main themes of this play, as Shakespeare explores how an honourable man can be driven to suspect his wife by someone with evil intent. As a Moor, Othello is an outsider in Venice. Iago's racism partly motivates him to convince Othello that his wife is being unfaithful, but perhaps it is Othello's outsider status which makes him believe Iago. In many of Shakespeare's plays, including *Much Ado About Nothing*, the 'honour' of women is seen as very important.

Romeo and Juliet
One of Shakespeare's most popular plays, and one of the most famous love stories of all time, *Romeo and Juliet* tells the story of two lovers who meet a tragic end because of their feuding families. Forced to deny their families and their names, Romeo and Juliet can't escape the violence that surrounds them. Shakespeare shows how fate and society can bring an end to even the strongest love.

The Tempest
Believed to be Shakespeare's last great play, this comedy tells the story of an act of betrayal 11 years previously. Like Hamlet, it's a revenge play, but this tale has a happy ending. Prospero forgives the brother who usurped him, and returns to Naples to become a Duke once more. At the end of this play, Prospero asks the audience to 'let your indulgence set me free', which is an instruction to clap!

Twelfth Night
Like *The Tempest*, this tale features a shipwreck (though this one happens before the play even starts). It separates Viola from her brother, Sebastian. Shakespeare liked to write about women pretending to be men, as he does in this play. The irony is that in Shakespeare's time, every part was played by a man, so Cesario's character would have been played by a man pretending to be a woman pretending to be a man!

For my mother, with love — A. M.

To my husband Will. In the words of another William,
"I would not wish any companion in the world but you."
— A. L.

Brimming with creative inspiration, how-to projects, and useful information to enrich your everyday life, Quarto Knows is a favourite destination for those pursuing their interests and passions. Visit our site and dig deeper with our books into your area of interest: Quarto Creates, Quarto Cooks, Quarto Homes, Quarto Lives, Quarto Drives, Quarto Explores, Quarto Gifts, or Quarto Kids.

A *Stage Full of Shakespeare Stories* © 2018 Quarto Publishing plc. Text © 2018 Angela McAllister. Illustrations © 2018 Alice Lindstrom.

First published in 2018 by Lincoln Children's Books,
an imprint of The Quarto Group.
The Old Brewery, 6 Blundell Street, London N7 9BH, United Kingdom.
T (0)20 7700 6700 F (0)20 7700 8066 **www.QuartoKnows.com**

A catalogue record for this book is available from the British Library.

ISBN 978-1-78603-114-3

The illustrations were created in collage

Set in Gill Sans Infant Std

Published by Rachel Williams and Jenny Broom
Designed by Karissa Santos
Edited by Katie Cotton
Production by Jenny Cundill and Kate O'Riordan

Manufactured in Guangdong, China CC052018

1 3 5 7 9 8 6 4 2